The Ghost of Fire Company 18

John B. Hicks

Quiet Man Publishing

ISBN: 0-9742829-2-8

Library of Congress copyright registration
TXu-1-215-511

Cover art by Miguel Romo

For more information, please visit us on the web at
www.quietmanpublishing.com

First Edition

10 9 8 7 6 5 4 3 2 1

Acknowledgements

To my family and friends that helped me with the book. Thank you for keeping the dream alive!

Other Books by John B. Hicks

My Buddypack

Divided World

Table of Contents

FOR THE FALLEN

Chapter 1
CONDEMNED

It was the summer of 1968 and the cement foundation of Fire Station 18 hadn't even dried before the engine company received its first alarm. A strong, steady breeze blew from the north, bringing with it the heat of the Mojave Desert. The weatherman called it a Santa Ana condition; the firemen called it trouble. Captain John Briggs, a twenty-year veteran of the department sat up front in his brand new 1967 Crown fire engine. With the wind swirling through his slightly graying hair, he navigated for Engineer Bobby Woods, guiding him street by street to the reported address. Not that Bobby needed the direction. Growing up in the area, he was very familiar with every street and curve in his district. Six feet tall and even grayer than his commander, he had learned to accept the man's help, even though he would give him directions to places where he had roamed as a child.

Seated behind Engineer Woods, watching the road go by from the view of his jump seat, sat Steve Forbes, the bull fireman of the company. "Bull" stood for the most senior member in the station. Slightly shorter than your average man, but with twice the spunk, years of breathing smoke and braving the endless parade of calls hadn't dulled his enthusiasm for the job. Arriving at the station a half-hour earlier than most, he started everyday the same: by cleaning up after the shift before. Sixteen men in one station made for one big mess—one that fireman Forbes couldn't tolerate. Even the rookies had a hard time keeping up with him. Rookies, or probationary firemen, as the department referred to them, were the new guys to the job. Usually young and full of willingness to do whatever it took to pass probation, they were the workers around the station—well, most of the time. Fireman Forbes turned his head and glanced over at the opposite jump seat where probationary Fireman Jim Kilpatrick sat. Two weeks new to the job, there was no mistaking the greenness that seemed to glow over him. Six-foot-one and heavy set, the pimples on his cheeks displayed his true age. Fresh out of college, where he had studied finance, Jim had felt the tremendous pressure of falling into the family business. Jim's father had been a fireman for the city, just as his father had, and his father before that. Jim's true dream, however, was that of starting his own accounting firm, wining and dining clients until all hours of the night. He wanted the good life that consisted of driving nice cars and vacationing in Miami Beach.

Reality soon sank in for Jim. With a little better than a C average in school, Jim found it hard to find a decent-paying job. After a number of failed attempts at employment, and a mounting student loan to pay off, he seized the opportunity presented to him by his father's friend, who, at the time, just happened to be in charge of the city's personnel department. Two months later and after successfully passing all the required tests, Jim Kilpatrick started the training academy. The academy, better known to the recruits as the drill tower, was ten long, hard, and frustrating weeks of putting up ladders and dragging hose across an endless yard of cement. Jim found the work physically and mentally challenging. Lifting a heavy wooden ladder up and down all day long while a drill instructor yelled in his ear took its toll on him. The kicker, however, that made him really question his decision to become a fireman, was the live fire drills. With temperatures reaching hundreds of degrees in what was little more than a well-disguised kiln, Jim was forced to enter a cement four-story structure in full turnouts (the protective jacket and pants firemen wear) along with forty pounds of gear strapped to his back. Arriving at the top floor via the staircase, the already exhausted trainee was then expected to put out a small fire in one corner of the room. Jim didn't know what the training captain's definition of a small fire was, but it sure wasn't the same as his. Jim would watch as the fiery beast would climb the wall of the structure, rolling itself violently across the ceiling. The sight of this, along with the intense heat, would drive the recruits to the floor as the nozzle man begged for permission to open the hose line. The nozzle man was the one at the front of the line, which also meant he was the heat shield for everyone else.

The temperature difference between the man in front and the personnel in the rear was sometimes dramatic. For some unknown reason, everyone forgot that fact, at least until it was his turn in the barrel. The poor person in front would not only take the brunt of the heat, he would also have to contend with the endless parade of pushing from behind. There, as many as five men, sometimes more, were all trying to get in and put out the fire. The only satisfaction the nozzle man would receive was when he actually put water on the fire. You see, smoke and flames were not the only things in a fire that the men needed to be aware of. The resulting steam from putting water on the fire was just as dangerous, sometimes delivering severe burns from the expanding gases. The steam, nonetheless, also helped put out the fire. The cooling water molecules would attack the fire, stealing one of the three main components it needed to live: heat. Fire, as most of us learned from our school visits to the local fire station, needs three components to support combustion: heat, fuel, and oxygen. This is known as the fire triangle. Remove one of the three elements and fire will cease to exist. Frankly, Jim didn't care how it worked, as long as the fire went out.

Now, with the basic training behind him, and a little prodding from his old man, Jim Kilpatrick finally graduated from the drill tower. Being a fourth generation fireman, Jimmy had a lot to live up to. Unfortunately, even before he arrived for his first day of work, he was already behind the eight ball. His father had been a pistol of a fireman, revered as one of the best. Reputation was everything in the department, and Jim was expected to carry on in his father's footsteps.

No matter how hard Jim tried, however, he would never be able to fill his father's shoes, and Fireman Steve Forbes knew this. Looking over at the rookie from the opposite jump seat, Steve Forbes watched as Jim nervously fumbled with the top button of his turnout coat. Steve yelled over at him, telling him to slow down and take it easy. His voice fell short, however, drowned out from the intense engine noise of the Hall-Scott motor. Most of the time there were three firemen who rode the tailboard, avoiding the engine noise altogether. But, because Jim was a rookie, and the other senior fireman was back at the station cooking, the captain felt more comfortable having the two firemen ride in the jump seats.

The infamous cooking detail. When one mentions the word cooking, he or she may first think it as a chore or as something mom had to do every night. Mom was not at the station, though, and to some men the chore of cooking was a passion; a passion with a reward. Besides being able to cook whatever he wanted, the fireman assigned the detail was exempt from doing housework and was always out of doing the dishes. He was also the one who chose the game after dinner to see who would do them. Some games for dishes were legendary in the fire department, from the infamous 99-card game to a round of putt-putt, a form of miniature golf played on the apparatus floor with a taped-up hockey puck and chalk drawn holes on the cement. Only his imagination limited a man from thinking up the crazy ideas to get his fellow firemen into the suds.

Chapter 2
FIRE SHOWING

As the two firemen sat anxiously in their jump seats watching the road fly past them, the captain suddenly called out the two words that sent excitement through every fireman's soul no matter how many times he heard it: "LOOM UP!"

"Loom up" was a term used by firemen to describe a visible column of smoke or flame showing from a distance. Steve Forbes quickly bent down and cranked his breathing apparatus open. The breathing apparatus or B/A as the firemen referred to it, was the fireman's fresh air supply. A thirty- or sixty-minute supply of compressed air, depending on the bottle size, was all wrapped up tightly in a metal tank. Along with a separate mask that attached to it, a fireman could enter a hazardous environment and breathe normally. Steve quickly unbuckled his seat belt, leaned across the engine cover, and spoke to Jim.

"Listen up, rook," he began. "We're going to be first in on this one. When we stop at the hydrant, I'll lay the line. I want you to jump on the tailboard and pull the running line. After that, don't you dare leave the old man's side. I'll be right up to help you two as soon as I can. Do you hear me, kid?"

Jimmy quickly nodded his head yes. He could do this, he thought. He had helped lay a line a hundred times before. They were all at the drill tower of course, but the act of connecting the hose to the hydrant, then racing off towards the fire was the same here as there. Engine 18 came to an abrupt stop and Captain Briggs called out the command to "lay a line." This order told the two firemen to get going and hook the hose up to the hydrant. Without hesitating, they jumped from their seats and raced to the back of the engine. Fireman Forbes unlatched the four-way valve, the piece of equipment that attached the hose to the hydrant, and swung it around hard. Forbes then quickly wrapped the hose around the hydrant so he wasn't pulled down the street when the engine pulled away, and then yelled loudly to the engineer to take off. The senior fireman watched anxiously as the engine roared towards the fire with Probationary Fireman Jim Kilpatrick hanging onto the back for dear life.

As the engine lurched forward, the rookie swiftly

moved to the right of the tailboard, narrowly avoiding the two-and-a-half-inch diameter hose as it poured out the back of the hose bed like a ribbon from a spool. Fireman Kilpatrick held on tight until the engine came to a complete stop some five-hundred feet down the road. After what seemed like an eternity to him, the sound of the air brakes hissed, signaling they had reached their final destination. As if someone had flipped the automatic pilot switch on, the intense hours of training that were brainwashed into each and every rookie suddenly kicked into high gear for Kilpatrick. He began to "pull the running line," part of the procedure for connecting the hose line coming from the hydrant to the pump of the engine. As he jumped down off the tailboard, he accidentally tripped on a hose coupling, falling face first to the ground. Shaken, he slowly got to his feet, and continued his duties of dragging the excess hose to the side panel of the fire engine. There, waiting for him, stood Engineer Woods looming over him like a downtown skyscraper. As if it was a plastic straw, Woods' massive arms grabbed the hose line from the rookie and proceeded to connect it to the side of the engine. Not more than ten seconds later, the flat lifeless hose swelled as Forbes, five-hundred feet away, opened the hydrant, sending a flood of water down through the line.

"Grab an inch-and-a-half hose line and get it to the

front door, kid," shouted Captain Briggs from the front of the engine.

Kilpatrick, doing what the captain asked, grabbed the nozzle attached to the hose lying in wait in the transverse beds, which was located on the side of the engine, and then turned towards the fire. Fear immediately struck the rookie's heart as he watched the flames soar from the large, multi-story commercial building. Excited onlookers observed as the fireman, already exhausted from all the excitement, struggled to pull the empty hose line around all the obstacles lying in front of the building.

Cars, forklifts, and crates filled the parking lot, partially obstructing the egress to the inferno, entangling the cotton hose, and making the job extra tough on the new fireman. Finally, after a few frustrating but exhilarating minutes, Kilpatrick completed the assigned task, and he now waited for the captain to join him.

It was a golden rule of the fire service—never, ever, go in alone. So even if Jim wanted to, he couldn't. As the rookie waited, Capt. Briggs made a few more radio transmissions on his walkie-talkie and then joined his rookie fireman at the entrance of the structure. Flames and heat licked at the firemen's ears as they prepared themselves for the battle ahead. They quickly turned on their air bottles and donned their breathing masks. Capt. Briggs looked over at the rookie, immediately noticing the young man's eyes, which grew larger and larger with every passing second as he stared at the man-made inferno they were all about to enter.

"Just stick with me, kid, and everything will be fine," assured the captain, trying to relax the anxious young man.

"Yes, sir," Kilpatrick quickly replied. "I'm okay," he continued, trying to hide his fear.

Suddenly, Fireman Forbes appeared at the two men's side, breathing heavily, the result of the long run from the hydrant. Not saying a word, the veteran fireman joined his co-workers, quickly donning his mask in unison with them.

"Okay, Jim," began the Captain, "Let's get this outside fire knocked down so we can get inside."

Jim steadied his back foot, opening the nozzle as commanded. A rush of cool air, followed by a heavy stream of water flowed from the tip. The rookie, struggling to maintain control of the hose line as hundreds of gallons a minute poured from the tip, quickly adjusted the stream for proper flow. This particular operation had to be done every time before actually fighting fire. If the stream was too wide, the water would just evaporate before it ever hit the seat of the fire. If too narrow, Jim and his crew would find themselves cooking from lack of protection. After a few twists of the nozzle tip, Jim eventually found the proper stream and began his work on the outside fire.

Sounds of men shouting filled the smoke-laden air as the truck men began their assault on the rooftop above. Jim paused a moment, looking upward at the truckees that were hard at work preparing to ventilate the fire. Truckees, as they were nicknamed, were the men assigned to a truck company. Most people knew the truck as the "hook and ladder." Their job was to put a ladder to the roof and then chop a hole in the structure to let the smoke and heat out from inside. This in turn would allow the men of the engine company easier interior access to fight the fire.

Jim continued his assault on the outside, swiftly knocking down the exterior blaze. Satisfied that the outside problem was now under control, the captain quickly took hold of Jim's shoulder, aggressively directing him towards the entrance of the structure. The rookie fireman noticed the change immediately. The once horrendous inferno that was just moments before spouting fire from its inner belly was now different. Taking the place of the glowing beast was now a much darker and ominous creature. Thick, black smoke poured from the entrance of the building, fouling the air with its pungent mist and blinding all who dared enter its entanglements of hidden dangers. Right off, Captain Briggs felt the resistance of his rookie as he nudged him forward towards his destiny.

"Come on, rook," yelled Forbes, "Get that line in there, and let's put this thing out!"

With a look of defiance, Jim shot a glance back at his fellow fireman standing behind him. Forbes swiftly returned the look with twice the fierceness, causing the junior member to quickly turn away. Knowing he didn't have much of a choice, Jim reluctantly followed the order, breaking the seal of the threshold with the tip of the nozzle. The smoke rapidly engulfed the men as they surged forward into the darkness. The heat was tremendous, immediately reminding Jim of his recent days fighting fires in the drill tower. The three men advanced the hose line blindly, Forbes taking up the rear, pulling up slack hose. They heard companies branching out from behind them in search of the seat of the fire. This brought some comfort to the rookie, at least knowing that they were not alone. Continuing their quest, the firemen progressed deeper into the structure. Sounds of crackling and popping surrounded them as they searched in what appeared to be the manufacturing part of the building. Tools and heavy equipment appeared in front of them, further obscuring the hunt for the fire.

Jim observed that the heat was now getting very

intense, yet there were still no visible flames. The captain continued to push him hard from behind, forcing the rookie deeper into the perceived danger. Panic started sweeping across Jim's body as his ears began to burn from the radiant heat. He tried to turn around, but the captain forced him frontward.

"What are you doing, Jim?" shouted Briggs through his face piece. "The fight is in front of us, not behind."

Jim didn't hear a word he said. The larger rookie again turned around, this time forcing the older man back. He tried to make his way past the captain, but just then, Fireman Forbes stepped up and helped force the rookie back.

"Jim, stop!" yelled Fireman Forbes, holding on tight to the rookie. "Just relax. We are right here with you."

By this time, Jim was far past the point of reasoning and wanted nothing more than to just get out of there. With all the strength he could muster, he pushed his body forward, breaking the grip of the veteran firemen. Before anything more could be done to stop him, the frightened rookie quickly disappeared into the smoke filled room. Briggs and Forbes attempted to follow him, however, it would be a useless gesture. During all the commotion, the fire itself had grown in intensity, driving the veteran firemen to the floor. Fighting for his life, Forbes immediately grabbed the end of the hose line and began to spray into the air.

Meanwhile, the panic-stricken rookie continued his way blindly through the choking smoke, heading himself deeper into trouble. Suddenly, off in one corner of the room, Kilpatrick thought he glimpsed an opening in the fog of danger. Hoping it was a way out, Jim turned and headed towards a dim light source. Unfortunately, he would be tragically wrong. As he opened the door to what he hoped was freedom from the nightmare, a rush of fresh air fueled the flames that now surrounded probationary Fireman Jim Kilpatrick. The last thing he saw was a great fireball rushing up to greet him, condemning his immortal soul for all eternity.

Chapter 3

THE BOOT

Katie Butler leaned gently against her kitchen table, sipping her hot coffee as she quietly read her newspaper on the morning of June 7, 2003.

"How time flies," she thought to herself, realizing the year was now half over.

However, what a half a year it had been for her. Only six months ago, Katie's life had been a lot different from the present. A recent graduate of college, where she had studied and received a bachelor's degree in fire science, Katie had spent most of her time driving up and down the state applying for a position as a firefighter. After stacks of applications and dozens of written tests, Katie finally received the letter she had waited half her life for—a letter of acceptance from the Los Angeles Fire Department. By January, Katie was starting the drill tower. Now for most recruits, the drill tower was filled with stress and hard work. Katie's experience was quite different from most. She still had all the stress involved, and no one could say she didn't work hard. She had an advantage over most of the other recruits however, the exception being the one that she now shared last names with, David Butler.

She was in love. And where love is, anything is possible. Katie had first met David at their orientation meeting for the department and hadn't left his side since. Unbeknownst to most of her class, especially the captains running the program, Katie and David started dating soon after that. The rest you could say is history.

"Good morning, Katie," greeted David, kissing his new wife on the back of the neck. "How did you sleep last night?"

"I've slept better," she replied, wiping the sleep from her eyes.

The smell of the newly brewed coffee filled the kitchen air, enticing David to pour a cup of his own. With his coffee in hand, he pulled out the chair next to his wife and sat down. He immediately grabbed for the sports section of the morning newspaper lying on the table, but Katie beat him to it.

"Hey, what's the deal!" he protested quickly.

"Have to be quicker than that, boot," she replied with a sheepish grin as she flicked open the paper.

Even though the two had been in the same drill tower together, Katie was still the senior firefighter around the house. Seniority on the department was established by the date you started the drill tower. Then, within each individual class, seniority was based on the sequence you were hired. Since Katie was hired third in her class and David tenth, Katie was senior. Now, when it came time to pick vacation, or when a vacancy at a station opened up, Katie would have first dibs on it. This drove David crazy, but he would never let her know it. He knew that like most firefighters, once Katie saw a weak point, she would exploit it for all that it was worth.

Admitting defeat, David grabbed the front page and grudgingly perused it. Katie smiled slightly knowing she had won. Ever since she was a small child, she had been filled with the drive to win and always tried her best to do so. Her dad had been the same way and had passed the trait along to his daughter. Finishing the last page in the section, she tossed the paper into David's lap.

"There you go, honey," she replied, now rubbing his shoulders. "Sorry about your Lakers. I guess the big guy missed too many free throws again."

The redness quickly rose up into David's face, but again he tried not to let her see his displeasure. He was upset because he had missed the basketball game on television. This was due to spending a good part of the night in preparation for an important drill that he had to present at work today. He had awoken this morning with the hope of reading the play by play of the game, but with the ending now spoiled, there was no need. It would be like eating a whole bag of sunflower seeds, only to have the last seed be bad, thus leaving that sour taste in your mouth.

Again, Katie smiled, knowing she gotten him once more. It wasn't that she was trying to be mean to him. It was just her way of having fun. Besides, if she didn't give him a hard time, he would soon start to wonder if everything was all right between them. Most people would think this behavior strange, however, not a firefighter. Like in most things in life, their sense of humor seemed to beat to a different type of drum. Around the station if someone wasn't pulling some sort of gag on you, things weren't right. If they teased you, they liked you. If they didn't, well, they didn't. Firefighters were notorious for practical jokes and nothing was sacred. Everything from finding your badge frozen in a bowl of water, to having your bedding hanging from the hose tower was fair game. No one was immune from the carnage.

One of the most infamous gags ever perpetrated on the department was played on a captain. The story goes that this particular officer fancied the lottery. Each week he would buy a ticket in hopes of striking it rich and retiring early. Like clockwork, every Saturday night he would turn on the television just in time to see the six little ping-pong shaped balls drop onto the rail, revealing the winning numbers. He would win five dollars here, a dollar there. He once even won fifty dollars. Nevertheless, the big one always seemed to elude him. His luck though was about to change; at least he would be made to believe so.

Unbeknownst to him, his crew had taped the lottery show a few weeks before. They then went out and bought a ticket containing those exact winning numbers. When they were asked to buy him a ticket while they were doing their daily shopping for mess, they just simply gave him that ticket. The plot was now set.

Saturday night soon rolled around with the captain being none the wiser. With the television and VCR on, the crew started the tape just as he walked into the room. The wide-eyed pigeon, believing he was watching a live broadcast, stared in amazement as one after another winning number somehow magically appeared on his ticket. Like a young schoolboy getting out of class for the day, the captain jumped up out of his seat as the last number was read. Yells and cheers emanated from his mouth as he danced around the station now thinking he was a millionaire. The crew joined in his celebration, playing the gag for all that it was worth. Unfortunately, even the best-laid plans can go terribly wrong, and this particular one was about to get real ugly. Regrettably for the unsuspecting crew, this individual captain did not get along with his superior, the chief. In the past, the captain had been very good at keeping his opinion to himself, but with all common sense out the door, and thinking this was his last day of work anyway, the captain proceeded to call his boss and tell him what he really thought of him. The crew sat there with their mouths wide open and hearts pounding a thousand beats a minute as their commander proceeded to enlighten his superior on his true feelings of him. Knowing the joke had now gone past the point of fun, the crew immediately stopped him mid-conversation and confessed their trickery.

To say the least, the captain was not amused. The scorned commander quickly apologized to his chief, playing it off as a misunderstanding. The chief, being a good sport, dismissed it as such and went about his business. The captain's crew would not get off so easy. Although particulars are not well known, the rumor is that midnight drills are still part of their daily routine.

Chapter 4
FIRST HOUSE

Katie stopped massaging her husband's shoulders, kissed him gently on his cheek, and then swiftly left the room, chuckling as she went. Moving down the hall, she dashed into her bedroom to ready herself for the day. The morning hour was passing quickly, and Katie didn't want to be late for her first day at the station. The sun was still tightly wrapped beneath the blankets of hills to the east as Katie hurriedly prepared for her departure. A normal workday for a firefighter begins at 6:30 in the morning. A rookie, however, was expected to be there much earlier. A lot of people don't know this, but a firefighter's schedule is very different from most other professions. Instead of working eight hours a day like the general public does, they work twenty-four hours at a time, usually doing twelve to fifteen days a month. Sometimes, that twenty-four hour shift can last an eternity. It is not uncommon for a firefighter to walk into the station at 6:30 in the morning and immediately receive an alarm. Then before they know it, it's already lunchtime, and they haven't even had a chance to shave. Some companies can run up to twenty calls a day, most lasting an hour in duration from start to finish. The fire department is a twenty-four hour, seven day a week business. They never close. Come Saturday, Sunday, Christmas, or New Year's, the stations are always staffed. Disasters do not take a day off, and the men and women of the department must always be at the ready. Many firefighters have spent the holidays on the fire-line while their family members are in the food line enjoying the celebrations without them.

With her hair combed and her bag packed, Katie made her way to the front door. David was already standing there, tapping his fingers on his watch.

"Let's go, girlfriend, time's a-wasting," said David.

"Keep your turnout pants on, cowboy. I'm moving as fast as I can," replied Katie, struggling with her bag as she attempted to eat a bagel on the run.

Katie breezed by her husband and headed for her truck. The cool summer morning held a slight chill in the air, evident by the sight of breath coming from Katie's mouth. She threw her bag into the back of her truck and climbed inside. David came along side and motioned for her to roll down her window.

"Now Katie, you play nice with the rest of the kids today. I don't want to get a call from the Principal saying otherwise," joked David, giving his wife a kiss goodbye.

"Don't worry, dear," she replied. "I'll be good. Let's just hope they play nice."

David watched and smiled as the window of her truck rolled up and she sped off to her first day at the station. The last thing he noticed before she drove out of view was the bumper sticker she had placed on her truck the night before. *Silly boys, trucks are for girls*, the sticker read.

"That should go over just great," thought David, climbing into his own car and heading off towards work himself.

Chapter 5

EVICTED

The city inspector fumbled with the assortment of keys attached to his ring. One after another, he inserted the metal instruments into the steel hardened lock, mumbling to himself every time they refused to turn. After about a minute of playing the match game, he finally stumbled across the correct one. The rusting mechanism grudgingly gave up its battle and sprung open. The inspector let out a sigh of relief as he proceeded to undo the thick metal bindings that secured the gate to the abandoned fire station. Why everything had to be a battle today he wasn't sure. His day had begun like that though, starting with the early morning call from his boss, telling him to get out to a job site and meet the fire department. He attempted to inform his superior that it was his day off, but the only reply he received was that of the dial tone echoing in his ear after his boss hung up on him. Quickly deciding it would be in his best interest to do so, he got dressed and set off to his assigned task. If he knew what really waited for him at the job site though, he would have never left the house.

Pushing open the now unlocked gate, the City Inspector walked alone into the compound of the abandoned fire station. The fire department representative was supposed to meet him at nine sharp, although he was nowhere in sight. The inspector optimistically thought he was probably just running late.

Wanting to get out of there as fast as possible, he decided to go in and open up the rest of the building. He glanced around the empty grounds, noticing old, dried leaves swirling around in a corner of the yard. Trash and other collectibles cluttered the rest of the perimeter, giving the place the appearance of a deserted wasteland.

"Boy, the economy must really be bad if they are considering using this place again," said the inspector.

Suddenly, out of a corner of his eye, a glimmer of light caught his attention. He quickly turned towards the distraction, noticing what he first thought was a man standing alone in the distance, the bright morning sunlight silhouetting his large body frame. Thinking the man was the fire department rep, he moved towards him, shading his eyes from the rising sun that was now directly in his sight. Blinking his eyes rapidly because of the bright light, the inspector soon reached the spot where he had first seen the man. When he got there, all he saw was empty space.

"I knew I should have grabbed a cup of coffee before I got here," the inspector said, scolding himself for not doing so. "Now, I'm starting to see things."

Without further incident, the lone inspector proceeded to open up the rest of the old structure, finding each door as troublesome as the front gate. Running out of patience, he looked down at his watch, seeing that the fire department rep was now a very irritating forty-five minutes late.

Opening the last of the doors, the inspector ventured inside the structure to look around. Spider webs and dust covered every inch of the building. Small packs of rats swiftly scurried around as the man made his way through their private domain. As he walked, the inspector tapped on the walls, quietly whistling to himself. The walls seemed to answer him back with a groan of their own, perhaps telling their unique stories of times long past.

Moving deeper into the building, a cold, dark feeling suddenly draped over the man. As if a thousand black widow spiders were running up his back, he could now feel the cold chill of the air churning its way through his crooked spine. Not quite understanding the dangerous situation he was now in, the man continued forward, moving even farther into darkness. Before he knew it, he soon found himself in the middle of what used to be the main crew's dormitory.

This large room with no divisions in it was the place where up to twenty men would try to sleep at night. With individual beds lined up on each side of the room, it took on the appearance of a bunkhouse at summer camp.

Suddenly, a flash of light dashed across the room in front of the inspector. Startled, the man fell backwards, landing on his bottom with a loud thud.

"What was that?" The man said trembling as he tried to stand up. He however, never got a chance to make it to his feet. The flash of light abruptly reappeared around him, this time taking on a more menacing appearance. Red and orange bolts of energy seemed to dart from within it, making their way through the man's body, quickly filling him with the feeling of impending doom.

The inspector next began to feel himself levitate off the ground, rising higher and higher into the cool morning air. He tried to break free of the force, but it was of little use. The cloud of light had secured him tightly, carrying him across the room as a puppeteer would carry his puppet. As the inspector unwillingly crossed the room, he immediately noticed the far window on the south wall slowly open. More panic flooded his senses as he realized what was about to happen. He swung his arms wildly, trying with all his might to slow his progress, yet the force did not yield.

Just like a cannon ball fired from a fortress, the inspector soon found himself flying out the open window, falling helplessly towards the ground below. Luckily, for him however, the force was not without concern for life. To what some would say was a perfect shot, the city inspector landed safely in a large trash bin below.

In a blink of an eye, the man jumped from the container, and ran full force towards the front gate. For the next two weeks, the city inspector's supervisor tried to reach him on the phone to try to find out what had happened, without success. The inspector never called in. He never returned to work. In fact, he was never heard from again.

Chapter 6

THE STATION

The first glimmer of light appeared over the horizon just as Katie pulled into the back of the station. She retrieved from her pocket the key that she had received from her captain a few days earlier when she had visited the station to drop off her gear and introduce herself to her new crew. This visit was customary prior to starting a new assignment. It helped to break the ice of being a stranger, and it also gave the guys a chance to size up the new rookie. She had brought with her the traditional gift of two gallons of ice cream, which was expected of all new recruits.

Katie quietly pulled into the back of the station, finding the gate to the parking lot unlocked and rolled open. She quickly found an empty parking space and pulled in. She gathered her personal belongings, along with a box of freshly baked donuts that she had picked up on the way, and walked towards the back door. This act of kindness was another long-standing tradition at a department built on tradition. Showing up to a new assignment without such a delicacy would have been a bad beginning for Katie.

The door to the station creaked as Katie slowly drew it open. Darkness still draped the interior of the building, with just a single light shining in a corner illuminating a large map on the wall. Katie crossed the apparatus floor, reaching the kitchen without incident. The kitchen at a fire station was generally the main living area for the crew. Everything around the station circled it. Next to fighting fires and saving lives, nothing was more important than eating. Without fuel an engine does not run. Without food, a firefighter doesn't either.

Historical pictures of past fires and firefighters long gone hung on the wall of the kitchen memorializing them. Two long, wooden tables occupied the one corner of the room. Next to them sat a series of benches for the firefighters to sit on. Situated on the opposite side of the room was all the cabinetry, filled with pots and pans and food alike. Two refrigerators and a large stainless steel stove encompassed the sidewall, along with a stainless steel sink. Attached to the south wall was a small, 27-inch television that hung from a bracket. This positioning allowed everyone to have plain sight of it, everyone that is except the rookie. Another long-standing tradition on the department was that rookies did not watch TV. At no time, except when watching a training video or cleaning it for inspection, was a rookie even supposed to be near one. They were there to learn, not to be entertained. If they had time to watch TV, then they weren't working hard enough.

Katie walked into the large room thinking it empty of personnel. Without hesitation, she flipped the light switch on, flooding the room with brightness. She next threw the dozen donuts onto the table, the cardboard box making a loud thud as it hit.

From the opposite corner of the room, Katie observed movement through an opening into the next room. This was the training room, at least that is what the department called it. To the firefighters, it was just simply the rec room. It was another large, rectangular shaped room, filled with a dozen or so recliners, and a big screen television. While it is a common misconception that the fire department supplies all these items for the firefighters, this is not the case. The fact is that almost everything of luxury at a fire station is bought by the firefighters for the firefighters.

Each and every day, every firefighter contributes a certain amount of money to a fund, which they call house dues. This money is used to help buy everything from shoe polish to shampoo, and even big screen televisions. To most firefighters, the fire station is their second home. They eat, sleep, and work there; most live practically half their lives at the station. That is why they occasionally need the little luxuries in life. Twenty-four hours can be a long time away from their actual homes.

The sound of the donut box hitting the table reverberated across the room and slipped into the ears of the sleeping firefighter crashed out in a recliner. With an instinctive reaction, the sleeping giant awoke to the sound of the box hitting the table. The need to feed immediately filled his senses. Without acknowledging Katie's presence in the least, the large figured man made his way over to the table and began feasting on the newly discovered treats.

Now, one would wonder why this man was sleeping in a recliner chair, when he should have been sleeping in a nice warm bed. Well, one would just have to take one good look at his belly and the reason for his sleeping location would be clear. At some fire stations, all the firefighters sleep together in one large room called the dorm. In such rooms, there are no walls separating individual beds, just a few feet of open space. One can only imagine the interesting sounds made in the darkness of the night. Most sounds are generally tolerated, however, snoring is not.

Such a person with this particular breathing pattern had two choices. First was to sleep in the dorm with the rest of the firefighters and face being pummeled with an endless supply of toilet paper rolls, a practice, although effective, that is against department policy. The second option was to sleep in the TV chairs as they are called and get a painless night's sleep. Katie stood and stared in amazement as the individual consumed his share, and perhaps someone else's share of the treats. She thought for a moment about saying something to him, but the thought of him mistaking her for another sweet morsel quickly changed her mind. With the utmost of care, the young firefighter slowly withdrew from the kitchen and headed for the locker room.

Now over the past thirty years or so, the fire service has seen a great change in the everyday life of a firefighter. This has been especially true at the station level. One of the main reasons for the changes has been caused by the introduction of women to the job. With their ever-increasing ranks, some of the old practices of life around the fire station had to change, one of those being the locker room arrangements. Being a female on the department wasn't always the easiest thing in life, but, it did have its benefits. Whereas the men would have one big room to share, which was filled with row after row of lockers, the women generally had smaller, more private quarters to call their own.

Katie made her way quickly over to the female quarters, trying to be as stealthy as possible. As she did, a sudden flash of light from behind caught her by surprise. She swiftly turned around to find another large figure of a man standing there, flashlight in hand, observing her. At first, she had thought the food giant from the kitchen had followed her to her lair, however, she quickly noticed that this figure was vastly different. Replacing the lifeless, dipping shoulders of the first man, were broad, strong cradles. Where the other figure's belly cast a large shadow to wherever it was pointed, this man's stomach seemed as tight as a knot tied to a boat dock. No, this was definitely not the same person, Katie was sure of this. As the glow of the flashlight diminished, Katie could now make out the face of her newly discovered guest. It was that of her captain, Ben Keller. Captain Keller, or Moose as he was nicknamed, was a gentle giant of a man himself. With a heart of gold, yet still possessing a firm control of command, Captain Keller was loved by all, yet feared by those who didn't respect the job.

"Good afternoon, Firefighter Butler," announced her captain, startling the woman.

"Afternoon, sir?" queried Katie.

"Well, it might as well be," replied Keller. "All I know is when I pulled up to the station this morning, I had to get out of my car and unlock the gate. Do you know how much I hate to get out of my car, Firefighter Butler?"

"I'm sorry, sir," she quickly replied.

"As you should be, Butler," the captain barked. "First thing you need to know about me is that I have three priorities in life; God, the department, and last, my car. I love my car so much that if I'm not at church or work, I'm in my car. Therefore, when I get to the station and find the gate locked, it means I have to get out of my car. Do you understand what I'm trying to tell you, Probationary Firefighter Butler?"

"I do, sir," answered Katie.

"Good," the captain replied, this time with friendliness in his voice, "then welcome to Fire Station 18."

With her heart beating a thousand beats a minute, Katie shook the man's outstretched hand and smiled. The older man returned the expression with a smile of his own, and then without saying another word, he turned and walked away. Katie let out a huge sigh of relief, taking her first lesson of rookie etiquette to heart. Next time she would make sure to beat him to the station.

Chapter 7
First Call

Katie continued on her way to the locker room, reaching it without further interruption. Quickly changing into her work uniform, Katie ventured back out onto the apparatus floor. She next gathered her turnout jacket and pants and headed for the fire engine. Opening the cab door located behind the captain's seat, she removed her relief's gear (the firefighter who worked the day before) and replaced it with her own. Next, she started opening each and every compartment of the engine, trying her best to memorize the contents. She went slowly, studying each piece of equipment inside very carefully. She proceeded like this because this was a very important exercise to her. This in fact would be her first mini-drill. During the probationary period of a firefighter, which typically last a year's time, the probationary firefighter is required to display his or her working knowledge of the job. This includes the ability to memorize minute details and locations of every piece of equipment and tool carried on the apparatus. This display of knowledge, typically expressed in oral presentation form, is called a mini-drill.

As Katie finished the inventory on one of the rear compartments, all the lights in the station suddenly came on. Next, a loud audible tone, followed by a computer-generated voice began speaking over the station's P.A system. "Engine company only, reported snake call, 12750 Balboa Blvd. Incident number three-fifty, response time, six-fifteen A.M."

For the second time this morning, Katie's heart-rate soared as the sound of the first call of her career blared in her ear. Two men she had met briefly the other night, followed by her captain, breezed by her and climbed on board the fire engine.

"Are you coming on this call, Rook?" Mike Phillips, the senior firefighter on the engine called out to Katie. "Or are you just going to stand there and wave goodbye."

Katie blinked her eyes rapidly, awaking herself from the surreal moment. Realizing she should be on the engine instead of standing there looking foolish, Katie sprinted for the cab and quickly climbed in. Sitting down, the rookie firefighter's senses went into overload as she took in all the external stimulation. The sound of the diesel engine roared as the engine pulled out onto the station's apron and slowly proceeded into traffic. Balboa Blvd was a large street, well traveled by cars. Speeds of sixty to seventy miles an hour were common to vehicles traveling on it and Engineer Stroud knew better than to just pull out and expect people to stop. In the olden days, red lights and sirens were enough to cause people to pull to the right of the road and stop. Now, however, in the age of cell phones and soccer moms driving mini vans loaded down with home theater systems, Engineer Stroud was cautious. Paul Stroud was a short, stocky man, with a barrel chest and arms to match. He consistently wore a warm smile upon his face, and was always joking around, never taking anyone or anything too seriously.

Cars slowly began pulling over to the right and stopping as the thirty-two-thousand pound engine bore down on them. Katie continued to stare forward, watching the road fly by at what seemed to her to be at break-neck speed. The engine, however, was traveling no faster than the posted speed limit. In years past, fire engines sped at high speed to reported incidents. With the invention of the personal injury attorney, however, along with written directives from the department, no apparatus traveled faster than the posted speed limit. Engine 18 was following protocol.

After about a minute of playing dodge ball with the traffic that occupied the large city street, Engine 18 arrived at the reported address of the incident. Katie immediately noticed an older gentleman sitting on top of a trashcan, his full body weight bearing down upon the metal container. The senior firefighter, Mike Phillips, calmly turned to Katie and told her to grab the snake catcher. This contraption was simply a long metal pole with a wire looped through the center of it. All one had to do to operate it was extend the loop part of the wire out the one end of the pole, then with the loop carefully positioned around the snake's head, they would just have to pull tightly on the other end of the wire sticking out the opposite end of the pole. This would act as a lasso, firmly securing the snake. If the snake was discovered to be a non-poisonous one, it was carefully bagged and relocated in a more suitable location, like a field or wooded area. However, if the snake turned out to be a rattler, which is about the only poisonous snake found in the area, it was swiftly destroyed, its severed head carried off and buried.

Katie jumped down off the engine and moved toward the back of the rig. She next climbed up on the tailboard, another name for the rear platform of the engine, and grabbed the snake catcher that was attached securely up top. Luckily for her, she had spotted the odd-looking device earlier while doing her morning inventory of the engine. Though it may seem a minor thing to most people, this was a major victory for a first house rookie. Most rookies couldn't find their own head even though it is attached to their shoulders. As Katie struggled with the bracket holding the snake catcher, Firefighter Phillips lazily walked over to the man sitting on top of the container.

"What's up, partner?" questioned the seasoned firefighter to the man. "What do you have under there, an anaconda?" Phillips chuckled.

The trashcan suddenly thrashed about, causing the older man to reposition himself. Phillips immediately stopped laughing.

"What do I look like, a zoo keeper?" the man replied with a southern drawl. "All I know is that it's big and you are going to need more people than just you and little missy over there." The man pointed at Katie as she neared him. "And you are for sure going to need more than just that stick she's carrying, unless you're just planning to make it mad."

"Okay, sir," Captain Keller said, getting into the conversation. "Why don't you just tell us what it looks like and then we can talk about what we need to deal with it."

Seeing the older officer dressed in all black and wearing shining insignias on his shoulders, looking and sounding as if he was in charge, the man on top of the trashcan turned his attention from Phillips to the captain.

"Well, sir," the man began, "I was taking out my garbage when all of the sudden I see this thing at least ten feet long and as thick as a small tree trunk slithering across my driveway. It was light brown in color with a huge lump in the middle of it.

"A lump?" asked Katie, not taking her eyes off the trashcan.

"I think that lump is Mrs. Wellston's cat," a small voice from behind Firefighter Phillips said. A young boy, about ten years of age suddenly appeared. "It's been missing for a few days."

"That would explain it not paying too much attention to me at first," the can man said. "I was able to get it under the trashcan pretty easily; however, it must not like the dark very much, because it sure has been trying hard to get out ever since."

"Well, we better get a look at what we are dealing with," Captain Keller said aloud. "Hey, Mike. Grab the pike pole and get ready to corral this baby."

The pike pole was a six-foot long fiberglass stick with a D-shaped handle on one end and a metal pointed end with a slight hook on the other. Generally it was used for poking holes in walls and tearing off roof tiles. Today it would be used for keeping distance between the snake and the firefighters.

Following the captain's direction, the old man atop the metal can jumped down and hurriedly put distance between him and the emerging reptile. At first, no one seemed alarmed. It looked harmless enough to the firefighters, its head poking under the can, exposing about a foot of its body. As more time passed though, the snake's actual size became unnervingly apparent. The old man's estimate of ten feet didn't even come close to the snake's true length. Fifteen feet was more like it, and that was being conservative. How, and more importantly, why this man risked life and limb to put a trashcan over this thing was beyond Katie. It appeared to be a boa constrictor—at least that was the consensus of the group. Probably a pet of someone's, at least at sometime in its life. Boas weren't known to be native to California. Captain Keller immediately started talking on his hand-held radio, calling the dispatch center for the appropriate resource.

"Okay, you two," the captain said, talking to Katie and Mike, "You guys keep this thing from escaping. I just called for that crazy Australian guy. He'll know what to do with it."

Like clowns in a three-ring circus, Katie and Mike circled around the reptile, poking and prodding it back to a safe distance. Katie obviously disliked reptiles, a fact that was very apparent to Mike. The senior firefighter thus took full advantage of this weakness, laughing aloud as he continuously lifted the snake's body with the hook of the pike pole and tossed it in the direction of Katie. After about five minutes of playing "keep the snake from escaping", a game that really didn't pose much of a challenge, due to the fact the poor reptile was carrying around what seemed to Katie to be at least a half a cow inside of it, the people from animal control finally arrived and took charge. Without incident, two older men dressed in light khaki uniforms simply walked up to the reptile, picked it up effortlessly and gently escorted it back to their truck. The stunned firefighters just stood there, not knowing what to say.

"Thanks for not hurting Clarence," one of the men in the khaki uniform said. "He just lives around the corner. His owner has been looking for him for about a week. It doesn't look like he has missed a meal. Though, it does look like we'll be getting a missing dog or cat call pretty soon. Anyways, thanks again."

The two firefighters continued to stand there, staring as the yellow animal control vehicle sped away, Clarence the snake now safely in their custody.

"Now, there's one call you will never forget," called out Captain Keller. "There is never a dull moment in the city. Right, Mike!"

"Right, Capt," replied the veteran firefighter.

"Okay, you two," continued the captain, "If we have had enough fun for today, let's get home. There's work to do and a job to learn for Firefighter Butler."

Chapter 8

A SINKING FEELING

"There is no doubt about it. I would estimate another inch this month," reported the civil engineer to the fire captain on the condition of the sinking apparatus floor of Fire Station 18.

This particular problem was first noticed six months ago while cleaning for annual inspection, which was an intense three-day period when all the big chiefs from downtown come by and make sure everything is clean and running right. As the firefighters cleaned, one of them noticed the apparatus floor separating from the wall. A civil engineer was soon dispatched to the station and determined that the station was indeed sinking. At the time, he stated that he would have to run some more tests and monitor the problem before determining the extent of the damage.

Now six months later, the bad news was in. The station would have to be closed and the crew relocated while the problem was fixed.

Katie rolled her eyes after overhearing the news of the impeding move. She stood outside the office with Robert Smith, another rookie firefighter as they polished the chrome running boards on the fire engine. Robert was working overtime or SOD as the firefighters referred to it. This three-letter acronym stood for "Special Overtime Duty." Katie scrubbed hard, trying not to think about the move as she made small, circular motions on the metal. She dreaded the thought of having to move to another station. This would only mean more work for her. For the past month, Katie had worked very hard around the current station, cleaning and scrubbing everything that she could find until it shined with her pride. Now, with the breaking news, she would have to start all over at a new place.

"So, Katie," began Robert with a quirky smile on his face, "Do you think they'll move you to old 18's while they fix the problem? I hear they've had people looking at it."

"I don't know," she replied with a quick snap. "What do I look like, a chief? That's why they get paid the big bucks to make those decisions. Wherever it is, I just hope it's clean."

"Not if it's old station 18," Robert continued. "That place hasn't seen a rookie since. . .," he hesitated for a second.

Katie stood there for a moment, waiting for him to answer. After about thirty seconds of silence, she couldn't wait any longer.

"Well?" Katie asked, "Are you going to tell me or are you just going to stand there and look stupid with that polish dripping down your pant leg?"

Robert Smith looked down to see that the bottle of metal polish had tipped over and that the liquid was now running down his pant leg like butter running down a hot stack of pancakes.

"Oh, man!" Robert yelled out as he stood up, spreading the polish even further down his leg. "This is my only pair of pants."

The rookie firefighter quickly ran towards the workroom to grab a rag, leaving the question about old Fire Station 18 hanging in the air. Katie quickly forgot about the subject, laughing to herself as she watched her fellow rookie run away in a panic.

The news of the move quickly spread throughout the station, and directives were given to pack everything that wasn't tied down. Not another word was spoken about the new place of assignment; however, Katie could tell by the mood in the station that there was something not quite right.

Moving day came quickly, and Katie hurriedly prepared to go. The moving trucks came without fanfare, and the firefighters, along with a crew of professional movers loaded them up quickly. After about two hours of hard work, the loading was finally done, and they were now ready to head off toward their temporary station. Katie jumped into the cab, sitting next to her regular partner, Mike Phillips.

"Hey, Mike," Katie began with a questioning tone. "Is there something I need to know about our new home? Ever since we found out about where we're going, everyone has been acting kind of funny."

"You mean no one has told you about old station 18?"

Mike seemed surprised. "I would have thought you would have heard about it from someone before this, you being at the new 18 and all."

Katie shifted in her seat when hearing this. She didn't like not knowing things that she should. And she definitely didn't like surprises. This particular phobia started when she was about eight years of age. Her brother Tim was a jokester. One day he thought it would be fun to surprise her by jumping out of the closet. He succeeded in his task, scaring her half to death. To her credit, she kicked him hard on his shin. For the next week, he didn't walk right. From then on, everything from creeping up behind her, to popping balloons, even surprise birthday parties were a no-no. Those who broke the rule paid the price. Her friends and family were well aware of how she felt about the subject. They all knew that if it were up to her, the word "surprise" would be completely removed from the English language.

After about a minute of bugging her partner, Mike finally agreed to tell her the story of old Fire Station 18. Katie sat and listened as he spun the fable of the rookie fireman that supposedly still haunted the walls of the old station. Cold chills ran across her body as the story unfolded. The more she listened, the faster she began to breathe. Soon, Katie found her hands cramping up, the result of her hyperventilating. Mike began to laugh as he observed the rookie squirm.

"Okay, Katie," the senior firefighter began, "I think you've had enough ghost stories for today. I don't want you going home sick. There's a lot to do today. And if you don't do it, I'll have to. Besides, it's only a story."

Hearing this, Katie relaxed slightly. Wanting to add one last jab before falling silent, Mike added just a little more.

"Don't worry, Katie. Everything will be just fine. Just

remember, no one has actually ever seen the ghost. At least no one that is still alive to tell about it, that is."

Mike Phillips let out a series of sinister laughs as he finished the comment, turning away from her just as they pulled up to their new temporary station.

Chapter 9
HOME SCARY HOME

Light replaced darkness as the old station began its second chance at life. A cool breeze began flowing across the apparatus floor, the result of the front and rear doors being opened after a long absence of use. The whole crew stood silently, watching the sunlight spread across the polished concrete floor. To every corner of the building it extended, making it not necessary to turn on any of the newly installed florescent fixtures.

In the old days, when everything was powered by man and not by machine, people knew how to design things to take full advantage of nature and its gifts. From its well-placed lot, positioned just right to receive the warming light of the morning sun, to its magnificently designed architecture that allowed for its maximum use as a fire station, old Fire Station 18 was a prime example of man's ingenuity.

Katie wavered as she struggled to carry a large box of pots and pans, and looked around at her new home at the same time. How beautiful she thought, viewing the large timber of the open paneled roof. There was no drop ceiling, no drywall, just real wood spanning the full length of the station. Reaching the kitchen without disaster, she dropped the cardboard box on the table and began her return trip to the moving van. As she pushed forward against the swinging kitchen door, she was instantaneously stopped in her tracks, unable to budge the door forward. She slowly backed up, expecting someone else on the other side to push their way through, but no one did. She called out, signaling to see if it was clear for her to proceed. There was only silence from the other side. Thinking someone was messing with her, she decided to go the long way around, cutting through the television room. When she exited the room onto the apparatus floor, she looked back at the kitchen door and found its passageway as clear as the day's sky.

"They can never cut me any slack," mumbled Katie to herself, referencing to the fact that the guys were always messing around, teasing her at every turn. "I won't be on probation forever," she continued, "and when it's over, watch out."

Katie made her way back to the moving van trying not to give it another thought. She found everyone still outside, milling around, talking about the new station. Even her partner, Mike, who was her prime suspect for the folly was there. He was inside the moving truck moving larger items around. She looked back at the kitchen door, then at him, and then shrugged her shoulders.

"Pretty good trick, Mike," she called out, catching her partner's attention. "You can move faster than I thought for an old man."

Mike turned around, giving the probationary firefighter a puzzled look. "What are you talking about, rook?" he replied. "Can't you see I'm working here? Are you going to jab at me all day, or are you going to get some work done."

Benny Rodriguez and Tony Dunn, the two firefighters assigned to the truck company started laughing. They had witnessed the exchange and couldn't help but put their own two cents in. "Hey Mike," called out Benny, "makes you feel just like home, hey buddy?"

Mike returned the comment with a wide smile, quickly narrowing it down to a dirty grin.

"Oh, and Mike," chimed in Tony Dunn not wanting to be left out, "Don't forget to carry her across the threshold. You wouldn't want to bring any bad luck to your new home."

Mike Phillips was about to respond to their comments when Captain Keller stepped up, putting an end to the bantering. "So what's the deal here, guys? Don't have enough to do, you two?" Keller shouted out as he came up behind the two idle firefighters, grabbing them by the shoulders. "Well, I can fix that. Follow me over to the other truck. I think I can find plenty of work for you."

The two firefighters' smiles quickly vanished as they realized they were caught red-handed, standing around doing nothing. Katie watched with a self-hidden satisfaction as the two bothersome men were hauled off to do their share of the work. She didn't smile outward though, for she knew she was on probation, and it was not her place to laugh. Mike, however, wore a well-deserved grin on his face, waving goodbye to the hecklers as they were dragged off. Again, Katie glanced at Mike, and then back at the kitchen door. She scratched her head now wondering if he was the true person holding the kitchen door shut, or if the real culprits were just pulled elsewhere. Katie then returned to her own work, not realizing she would be wrong on both accounts.

Now, with everybody helping, the moving trucks were quickly unpacked, and the station soon took on the appearance of a work place instead of a graveyard. As the day continued, and without much notice to the workers, the sun silently traced across the brilliant sky, soon retiring to its resting place in the western horizon. Dinnertime came and went, and the exhausted crew promptly settled in for what most hoped would be a slow and quiet night. Katie found a small niche upstairs for herself next to the dorm. It wasn't very big, only about five-feet square; nevertheless, it was large enough for her to find some solitude of her own.

Not everyone at the station had intentions for a quiet night. Benny Rodriguez and Tony Dunn had not easily forgotten their earlier chastising, followed by the rigorous work detail given to them by Captain Keller. To them, the encounter with Katie and Mike Phillips was the reason. Not that they held a grudge against their co-workers, for deep down inside, Benny and Tony knew if you play, you must sometimes pay. It was just part of the game. They had no intention, however, of letting a first house rookie get the best of them. No, it was payback time, and old Fire Station 18 would again play host to it.

Chapter 10
LET THE GAMES BEGIN?

A probationary firefighter has many responsibilities around the station. One of those was making sure he or she was always the first to do what needed being done. If the doorbell rings, be the first to answer it. If the dishes need washing, be the first one to finish your meal and do them. If the alarm bell rings, be the first one on the engine.

There was nothing more humiliating than letting a veteran firefighter beat you to the punch. Thus, the rookie always had to ensure that they were the closest to things, jockeying for the best position at all times. This was especially true when it came to the sleeping arrangements. At night, when those lights came on and the alarm sounded, Katie would have to be the first one to the fire pole for the slide down to the ground floor, or she would risk being left behind. This meant having the bed closest to the pole hole. This also meant she was the prime candidate for one of the oldest jokes on the fire department: the bedding down the "pole hole" trick.

The way it worked was simple. As the poor, unsuspecting victim slept, a strong, thin line was tied to one end of his or her bedding. The other end was then carefully tied to a section of rolled hose. With this accomplished, all one now had to do was stealthily make his way to the pole and push the section of hose down the hole. Before the victim would know it, all fifty feet of hose, along with their bedding would vanish below, making for one very rude awakening.

The redness of the digital clock's numbers burned through the darkness of the dorm, announcing the eve of the next morning. Twelve o'clock a.m. sharp showed on the display. The crew had finally retired to their bunks after a hard day's work. The sound of sleeping firefighters filled the air as a chorus filled a church on Sunday morning. Not all were sleeping, though. No, it was time for the two scorned firefighters to play their trickery. Carefully and quietly, Benny and Tony climbed from their beds and headed downstairs. As they left the dorm, Benny glanced over at Katie, seeing her fast asleep in her bed. He then flashed a quick look at the pole hole. A slight smile formed on his lips as he left the dormitory.

As Benny entered the locker room, nature called out to him. He quickly decided to make a quick pit stop at the bathroom before going downstairs to begin the night's adventure. He signaled to Tony to proceed with the mission, telling him he'd be right with him after he finished. Understanding, Tony nodded his head and then disappeared around the corner. With his partner's acknowledgement, Benny proceeded to the bathroom, which was at the far end of the locker room. As his ankles snapped and knees popped, the results of long hours on the fire lines and twenty extra pounds around his waist, Benny made it to the bathroom without incident. Heading for the first stall, he entered, locking the door behind him.

As he sat alone in the dark, he immediately noticed the coldness emanating from the white tile floor, making the seasoned firefighter's toes curl. Suddenly, and without warning, a bright flash of light engulfed the bathroom stall. Benny immediately covered his eyes, the brilliance of the light temporarily blinding him.

Meanwhile downstairs, Tony was hurriedly preparing the hose, securely tying the rope around the rolled section. As he did so, he also felt the temperature of the station suddenly drop, the sight of his own breath becoming visible as his respiratory rate quickened. For a moment, he stopped manipulating the rope, giving his changing surroundings a good look. He watched as crystals began forming on a small puddle of water lying beneath the drinking fountain that had been slowly leaking ever since it had been turned on. Tony quickly stood, a feeling of uneasiness overcoming him. With caution, he walked over to the fountain and stepped onto the mini glacier with his size 11 boot. Effortlessly, the newly formed ice immediately broke away under his body weight, sending the sound of cracking ice echoing across the apparatus floor. A wave of shivers followed, racing down Tony's spine like a freight train on a downward pass. It was nothing, however, compared to what he would hear and see next.

The brilliance of the light was mesmerizing, yet frightening at the same time. Tony stood motionless, staring up at the top of the staircase as the light poured out of the passageway. A noise, almost human-like, yet too terrifying to be so, emanated from the glow. The thought of escape flooded Tony's senses. He quickly found himself paralyzed with fear and could not move; a strange thing to happen to a man with ten years of running into burning infernos. Then it suddenly appeared. It was only for a second, but still it was there. A man, at least he thought it was a man, large in stature, yet young in appearance. He was wearing some sort of uniform that Tony didn't recognize, although it was somewhat familiar to him. Then as suddenly as he appeared, he quickly disappeared, along with the bright light and eerie sounds. Left in his place was the larger outline of Benny Rodriguez standing silently at the top of the staircase, his face as white as a ghost.

Chapter 11
HELPING HAND

It starts with the lights coming on, soon followed by the low intense tone that gets louder and louder. It was the sound of an alarm coming into the fire station late that night. At first, Katie thought she was dreaming, still thinking she was back at home in bed, her husband turning on the lights for one of his late night runs to the bathroom. However, after a brief moment of disorientation, the realization that she was still at work caught up to her. She quickly sprung into action, jumping out of bed, and making her way speedily to the pole hole. Still half asleep, she grasped the metal pole with two hands, followed by her feet wrapping around the bottom of it. With more speed than she intended, she spiraled downwards towards the ground, stopping abruptly before impact. She then gently put her feet to the ground and moved out towards the engine. As she did so, something very odd caught her attention. In fact a number of odd things did. The first thing she noticed was Tony Dunn sitting on the ground, staring upward with a blank expression on his face. Next, she saw Benny Rodriguez at the top of the staircase, standing motionless, a white, pale look washed across his. Knowing Benny and Tony so well, these two things put together normally would not mean much to her, but the third thing was definitely not the norm. There, in the corner, floating about five feet off the ground she saw him or what she thought was a him. He was about twice her size, she estimated, with brown wavy hair, wearing what looked like to her to be an old pair of turnouts. He just floated there, a faint luminous glow around him. Upon his face, he wore a expression of longing. Stunned, Katie stopped and did the only thing that came to her mind—she waved. Unexpectedly, the vision waved back thus causing her heart to skip a beat. She quickly put her hand down, her eyes blinking rapidly. A thousand things ran through her mind. Was she dreaming this? Could she still be nicely tucked in bed, fast asleep, all of this being the result of that last piece of chocolate cake she ate before going to sleep? Her husband often warned her of the effects of chocolate. He said it made her goofy. She thought it just made her feel. . . well, happy.

She pinched herself hard, quickly feeling the pain.

"Ouch," she said aloud, thinking the stimulus felt like she was awake. She then rubbed her eyes vigorously, trying to get all the sleep out of them. Looking up at the vision again, she discovered him still there. "Well, that didn't do it," she said. Maybe she wasn't dreaming. Maybe he was real, but a real what? A thought quickly came to mind, and almost immediately, but unsuccessfully, the reasoning part of her brain tried to shut it out.

"A ghost!" the words quietly parted from her lips.

The vision in the corner began nodding his head. This unexpected reaction sent a cold chill through her. Suddenly, a large shadow loomed over her, again startling her.

"What are you doing, Katie?" her partner, Mike Phillips said, passing by her and climbing onto the engine. "Let's go, we have an auto fire."

Still shaken from the sight of the vision, she hesitantly made her way over to her side of the engine and climbed in. She found Mike inside, putting on his turnout coat. She immediately started to do the same, fumbling at the task.

"What's wrong, kid? Bad dream?" Mike questioned her from his side.

Katie didn't answer him. She just continued to put on her protective gear, staring out her window as she did. Then, from the corner of her eye, she saw it again. With an effortless-like flight of a glider, the ghost, at least that is the only thing she could think it could be, flew towards her. The glowing specter passed by her, stopping at the tailboard. Almost playfully, it looked at her and winked. It then disappeared around the back of the engine just seconds before the emergency vehicle departed the station.

The twenty-two-ton engine roared down the street, its sirens signaling to all that it was approaching. Even though he was half-asleep, Engineer Stroud drove to the reported address as if he was on autopilot, not missing a single turn. Making his way onto Chatsworth Street, Mike Phillips looked to his left, and then called out to his crewmates, "Loom Up." And there it was. Not a huge loom up, but still quite impressive for Katie since she didn't have much experience. It almost made her forget what she had just seen—almost. Not that she was sure at all about what she had just witnessed. "Was it a ghost?" she wondered to herself again. Or was it just the residual of a nightmare she was having prior to the call. She wanted to tell her partner but resisted the urge, fearing he would think she was crazy. And he would probably be right. There were no such things as ghosts. Those were things of fairly tales and campfire stories, not real life. She was now a Los Angeles firefighter responding to an auto fire, not a girl scout sitting around a campfire on a mountain outing telling scary stories.

The engineer made one last turn as the captain checked his map for the closest hydrant, just in case they needed extra water. This was not always necessary since a fire engine doesn't always need to connect to a fire hydrant for water. Built right into the engine is a self-contained tank that can hold up to five-hundred gallons of water. If used properly, it can put out a lot of fire. Depending on the size of the hose line used by the firefighter, the water supply could last as little as thirty seconds or as long as twenty minutes.

Not long after spotting the loom up, the engine arrived on a vacant street well known to the firefighters as a dumping ground for car thieves. There, they discovered a Volkswagen van fully involved in fire. Flames and smoke poured from its windows. It was thick, black smoke, the kind that once exposed to, would continue to invade one's smelling senses for a week. Mike jumped off the engine first, followed by Katie on the other side. Katie went straight for the hose line, while Mike grabbed the dry chemical extinguisher. The "dry chem" as it was called, was an excellent firefighting tool. With the ability to put out a large amount of fire, it is often used as a safety back up on auto fires and anything involving flammable liquids.

With the hose line in place, and Mike backing her up with the dry chem, Katie began her assault on the fire.

First checking for the proper water stream, she then fully opened the nozzle. The velocity of the water coming from it pushed her slightly back; however, by shifting her weight forward, she was able to advance towards the car. The smoke and flames continued to pour from the inside of the van as Katie shifted side to side trying to extinguish them. The captain grabbed the Hayward, which was a metal prying tool, and walked over to the back of the van. He carefully lifted the rear hatch open, revealing the engine compartment. Most cars had the engine in the front, but the Volkswagen van's engine was located in the rear.

"Watch this, Paul," said Mike to the engineer as he walked over to Katie. "Hey, boot," he said trying to hide his excitement. "Get that nozzle over here and hit the engine compartment."

Mike quickly grabbed her by the shoulders, pulling her back. When he had her positioned at a safe distance, he released her and let her return to the task at hand. All three veteran firefighters knew what was going to happen next. They stood silently, not saying a word to the rookie, the anticipation building within them with every passing second. Then it happened. For a brief second, night became day as the water hit the hot magnesium engine block sending sparks flying in all directions. They were white, blistering sparks, as bright as any fireworks on the Fourth of

July. This was one of the oldest tricks in the book played on rookies. Most had never heard of a magnesium engine block, or knew that once it started to burn, that water only made it worse, intensifying the flame and sending small chucks of white hot metal flying in all directions. The only way to put it out was to hit it with a heavy stream of water from a safe distance and break it into smaller, more manageable pieces.

Seeing the shower of sparks, Katie quickly retreated backwards, tripping herself up on the excess hose lying on the ground. She fell hard, sailing towards the asphalt like a missile. Mike's stomach tightened as he watched his partner tumble. At the time he set her up, it seemed like a good idea. The same trick was played on him when he was a rookie, just as on thousands of rookies before him; however, he wouldn't have done it if he knew this was going to happen. The three veterans continued to watch, helpless to stop her descent. It was all happening very fast, yet to them and to Katie, it all played out in slow motion.

Then, something unexpected happened. Just milliseconds before Katie hit the ground, her body abruptly stopped mid-air. She floated there, motionless as the rest of the company stared in amazement. Not knowing what to do, they continued to look on as their fellow firefighter's body then went almost horizontal, somehow levitating some two feet above the ground. Not exactly sure what had happened, a relieved, yet stunned Katie quickly turned her head to see who had caught her, but she saw no one there. She immediately reached back, trying to grab a hold of something solid, yet her arms passed through empty space. "How could this be?" she thought. She could feel what felt to her to be strong arms holding her but could see nothing. She glanced over at her crew, noticing the same look upon their faces that Tony and Benny wore when she left the station. She shot them a questioning look, but all they responded with was a shrug of their shoulders in unison.

Suddenly, the vision that she had seen earlier in the station appeared. He stood there above her, his arms gently cradling her as if she was an infant. He wore a pleasing smile upon his face as the two exchanged looks. Then, with the gentleness of a father laying his baby down to rest, he slowly released her to the ground and then vanished into thin air.

Chapter 12
REMNANTS

There weren't many things that made a firefighter speechless, but one could have heard a pin drop on the ride home to the fire station. With the auto fire extinguished, Engine 18 headed for the barn, everyone safe, yet not sound. All four firefighters were visibly shaken, no one more so than Katie. They had all seen the vision, the ghost, or whatever it was. Katie though had felt it pass right through her soul. And when it did, something else unexpectedly happened. It left something behind—something of itself. Rolling down the window, Katie could feel it deep inside her. The overwhelming feeling of loneliness echoed throughout her, the results of the remnants left by the ghost. Yes, ghost. She now knew what it was, and there was no doubt about its true identity.

The engine pulled up to the station, Mike jumping off first, taking traffic control. Katie exited on her side of the engine, making her way to the tailboard. With all obstacles clear, she reached up and quickly pushed a button that was located on the back of the engine two times. This in turn, rang a buzzer inside the cab, signaling to the engineer that it was safe to pull forward. When the engine was positioned right, she then pushed the button three times, telling him it was safe to back into the station. As the engine moved backwards, Katie kept her finger on the button, ready to push it once hard, if she needed the engineer to stop for any reason.

With the engine company safely back in the station, its crew, along with the rest of the members of Station 18 gathered in the kitchen. The shock of the earlier incident with the ghost had worn off for Tony and Benny, and the two had awakened the rest of the firefighters, spinning them a fantastic story. Not used to waking up at night, the members of the truck company were not amused at their tale. Tony and Benny were only seconds away from being hung by their ankles from the hose tower when the engine company had returned home and confirmed their findings.

"You're telling me a ghost is running around my station without my permission," Captain Wally Houston, the Task Force Commander, shouted out.

Wally Houston was a tall, thin man. Fair, yet stern, the

gray in his hair and the wrinkles about his eyes and face told the story of the fifty-nine year old task force commander. The Task Force Commander was the man in charge at the station. He or she held the rank of Captain Two.

A slight promotion from a Captain One, this Captain rode on the truck, or hook and ladder as it was called. When the engine runs a call alone, it is called an engine. When the truck runs a call alone, however, it was called a light force. The "Light Force" was a combination of a truck apparatus and a pumper engine. Where the truck went, the pumper followed. This is because the truck doesn't carry any water, only ladders. Put all the companies together: the engine, truck, and pumper, and the result would be a task force.

The members of Station 18 stood silent, not knowing how to answer Captain Houston. After an awkward few seconds, Katie finally spoke up.

"I believe he thinks it is his station, sir," the rookie firefighter responded.

Shocked, the rest of the crew turned and stared at Katie. The embarrassed firefighter turned slightly red, but did not retreat in her stance.

"So he does, does he!" the Captain Two replied, giving her the evil eye. "And how do you know this, may I ask?"

Feeling the courage building inside her, she gathered all her strength and replied to him, "I can just tell, sir. Don't ask me how, but I can."

Hearing this, Benny and Tony started to laugh in the corner. Captain Keller immediately came to her defense.

"You know, you two," he began, "I saw this young girl come face to face with this thing, and she stood her ground. Okay, maybe she floated above the ground, but she held her own. Now hearing your story, I say it was a lucky thing that one of you was in the bathroom at the time, and the other, well, let's just say it is a good thing the city gives you more than one pair of pants."

Hearing this, the rest of the crew started laughing. Benny and Tony cringed at the ridicule, quickly turning their attention towards Katie. If looks could kill, there would now be two ghosts in the station. Katie turned away, pretending not to see the two firefighters burning a hole through her with their eyes.

Trying to defend his manhood, Tony immediately replied. "Hey, I wasn't afraid."

Then, not wanting to look like the weak one, Benny, promptly chimed in his own response. "Yeah, I wasn't scared. It just caught me off guard, that's all. I promise if I ever see it again, it will be a different story."

"Yeah, whatever," Katie's partner, Mike called out.

"Big words, from a big man, and I don't mean tall, either," Mike referring to Benny's waist size.

"Oh yeah," replied Benny, standing up and heading for the door. "I'll prove it. Let's go get this thing. No one's going to scare me out of my house, especially not Casper."

Feeling his energy, the rest of the crew stood and followed him out of the kitchen. Like kids playing Cowboys and Indians, Benny and his fellow firefighters hooted and hollered as they made their way over to the truck and pulled out their axes. The captains tried to stop them, but soon figured it would be easier to join them and supervise, rather then to try to change their minds. Besides, they wanted to have some fun too.

Everyone's blood was hot and flowing, except Katie's. She stood at the doorway to the kitchen, shaking her head in disgust. One of the greatest discoveries of the twenty-first century, she thought, and all they wanted to do was to hack it to death, which, of course would be impossible. It was already dead. Overlooking this realization, the mob of would be hunters started to make their way upstairs, their axes at the ready position.

Suddenly, as if they had just walked into a freezer, the air around them became unsettlingly cold. Benny immediately stopped his forward motion, quickly noticing the telltale sign of trouble around them as the sight of their individual breaths again became apparent.

"Oh, oh," Benny called out, taking a few steps back.

Slapping his hand hard on Benny's shoulders, Mike pushed his fellow firefighter forward, quickly stopping his retreat. "Now where do you think you're going?" the senior firefighter replied. "What happened to 'Let's get Casper!' You're not changing your mind, are you?"

The force of the slap on his back startled Benny, making him swing around hard to face Mike.

"I'm not changing anything," replied Benny, the nervousness apparent in his voice. "I was just formulating my plan of attack."

Not believing his story for a moment, Mike and the rest of the crew gave him a doubtful look.

"No, really, I was." he protested. "I thought we could. . ."

He never finished the sentence. With lightning fast speed, Benny's axe, along with the rest of the groups tore from their hands. They flew across the apparatus floor, landing neatly in a stacked pile. The men, paralyzed with fear, froze in place. They would not stay in that position for long. Their host had different plans for them. Just as their axes had moments before, the men began to levitate off the ground. One by one, they slowly rose off the steps, spinning as they did. The higher they went, the faster they spun.

Katie, still immune from any of the frolics, watched with slight humor from the safety of the apparatus floor as her crewmates floated above her. She listened as the earlier sounds of hooting and hollering changed to screams and yells, Benny and Tony seeming to be the loudest. Then, as quickly as they lifted into the air, the floating firefighters soon found themselves again the victims of gravity. Downward they went like missiles, each of them landing in different locations. Luckily, Mike landed in a soft hose bed, along with the two captains. Others found themselves not as fortunate, hitting the solid concrete of the apparatus floor. Tony landed on top of the engine, hitting the metal roof hard. Steve Wish, the apparatus operator who drove the truck, ended up on top of a storage bin, covering his clothes in an inch of thick dust. Benny though, being the ringleader of the group paid the heaviest cost of all. Unfortunately, for him, he had somehow managed to float right above one of the oil bins, which just happened to be full at the time.

Benny's eyes grew large as the top of the can came off, exposing the liquid below. As the spell of flight wore off, he fell from the sky, head first, into the barrel. He rapidly emerged from its depth, looking more like a sea lion than a firefighter.

Seeing the veteran firefighter dipped like an ice cream

cone, Katie couldn't help but laugh. She looked around the station, seeing her co-workers spread out across the apparatus floor, attempting to wear off the shock. She walked over to the engine, putting her hand out to Captain Houston who was climbing down from the hose bed. His legs were shaky, and his skin was slightly pale, but he did his best to hide his condition. Her other captain, Ben Keller, didn't look much better, but he waved her hand away, electing to climb down on his own power.

"What in the world was that?" asked Captain Houston, now a little more steady on his feet.

"I don't know, sir," replied Mike Phillips as he came around from the front of the engine. "But, whatever it was, I don't think it's from this world, at least, not anymore.

"It was from this world, sir," called out Katie, this time her crew listening to her. "And I think it was once one of us."

"You mean a man?" inquired Tony Dunn, holding his side that he hurt in the fall.

She turned towards Tony answering him. "Yes, a man," she said with authority. "But, more importantly, I think he was a fireman."

Silence gripped the station. For a moment, Katie thought they didn't believe her, a dumfounded look washing across their faces. However, their blank looks soon turned into that of awareness as the memory of the past stories came flooding back to them. They had all heard the tales—the ones about the rookie fireman who supposedly haunted the station after dying in a fire years ago. Some rumors blamed the captain, putting his crew where they shouldn't have been. Others, however, tell a different story of a rookie firefighter that should have never been assigned to a station.

Chapter 13

A NAME FROM THE PAST

"His name was Jim Kilpatrick," Katie whispered aloud as she went through an old commemorative fire book she had found in the station's library.

"Did you say something, dear?" asked her husband, David, as he watched TV, the two sitting on the couch together.

It was now the following morning after the ghostly encounter. Katie and the rest of her crew had gone home, not mentioning a word to the oncoming shift about the ghost. They figured they would just laugh at them, not believing a word they said; so they just went home silently. To be honest, they still didn't believe it themselves. Yes, some of the crew had seen the ghost, and all had felt its presence, but the reasoning side of their brains still wouldn't allow them to believe it, at least not fully. Katie however, not suffering from amnesia, had no problem believing in him. She now knew what he was, and most importantly, who he was.

"So, how was your night, Katie?" David asked, flipping the channels on the television. "We got up once for a dumpster fire, but that was it," he continued.

A startled Katie looked up from the book she was reading. She was pale in the face, with droplets of light sweat trickling down from her forehead. She had just finished a short excerpt from the book about the night Jim Kilpatrick died. It had only taken her a minute to read the article, however, in that short period of time she had somehow managed to relive the complete incident, seeing everything, right down to the realistic details of his end.

"You okay, babe? You're not looking so good," asked David, turning off the television and putting his hand on his wife's forehead.

Katie quickly grabbed his hand and pulled it away. Surprised at her reaction, David backed away from her, giving her some room. Katie, realizing what she had just done, lunged at her husband, holding him tightly.

"What is it?" asked David, his pulse quickening. "What's wrong?"

Katie was now sobbing with her face buried in his

shoulders. He pulled her from him, looking deep into her eyes. He saw nothing but despair in them.

"Come on, Katie, you're starting to scare me. What gives?"

Wiping the tears from her eyes, Katie did her best to compose herself. "Do you trust me, David?" she asked, watching his reaction carefully. "And haven't I always told you the truth?"

"Yes," he replied, his voice not wavering. "I believe you have. Why?" He took his hand and ran it through her hair. This relaxed her some. "Just tell me what's going on here."

Searching for reassurance in his eyes, she gave him one last look. Finding what she needed, she took a deep breath and told her story. David listened quietly as she went through the whole thing. From the auto fire, to the station incident, she even showed him the article in the book. She held nothing back.

Mentally and physically fatigued, Katie finished her saga, and then collapsed on the couch, throwing her arms above her head. There, she sat and watched her husband carefully as he digested the new information. For a moment, David didn't say a word. He just sat there motionless, studying her face. Katie could see the struggle within him. Did he believe her story, she wondered. She couldn't blame him if he didn't. After all the practical jokes she had played on him in the past, it would be hard for anyone to believe, especially with a crazy story like this.

Not wanting to leave any doubt in his mind, she decided to show him one last thing to convince him.

"I know it is hard to understand. Trust me, I didn't want to believe it myself at first, but I need you to believe me now. Pulling the bottom of her shirt up, she exposed her stomach to him.

"You know the birthmark I have. The one I hate to show anyone. Do you remember the color of it and how dark it was? Well, now look at it."

He moved nearer to her, taking a closer look at the heart-shaped mark he had seen a thousand times before. This time, however, it looked different to him. The once dark, almost black mark was now a bright red, shining with a brilliance of a freshly cut ruby.

The immediate expression change on his face signified to Katie that he was now a believer. He slowly ran his fingers across the birthmark, making Katie squirm.

"Stop it, it tickles," she said slapping his hand away.

A thousand things raced through his mind as he continued to ponder the situation.

"But how is this possible?" he asked shaking his head, still struggling with the truth.

"Don't ask me," she replied. "I'm just as confused as you are. However, ever since he passed through me, I can't help but feel connected to him in some way. As a matter of fact, I can feel him right now!"

Hearing this, David immediately jumped back from her. Katie shook her head, laughing some.

"I said I can feel, not see him, you knuckle head." Katie then explained. "He's not here right now. I just can feel, well; what he is feeling inside, his emotions."

Hearing this, David relaxed and again moved back towards his wife; this would be a mistake on his part. Sensing a more relaxed atmosphere, and feeling better about the situation, the mischievous part of Katie's mind quickly went to work.

Still feeling some slight hesitance from him, Katie thought she would have some fun and mess with him a bit. As he neared her, she quickly stiffened her posture and whipped her head back, closing her eyes tight. She next raised her hands slowly and began mumbling softly. The hair on the back of David's neck rose like the morning sun as he again pulled back from her. Katie continued the possessed like actions as David struggled to hear what she was saying. Gradually, Katie's voice raised in volume as David retreated in his position. Finally, after about thirty seconds of hearing the same sounds repeatedly without being able to make out any intelligent words, David at last clearly heard what she was trying to say.

"My husband David is a big scaredy cat!"

Seeing the expression change on her husband and knowing he had finally heard her, Katie started laughing as David bent his head in defeat.

"Don't worry, dear," Katie began, "We can sleep with the lights on tonight if you like." She then swiftly moved towards him catching him with his head still down. With the grip of a wrestler, she wrapped her one strong arm around his neck and proceeded to rub her knuckles on the top of his head with her other.

"Okay, okay," he pleaded as the pressure of her hand increased. "I admit it, I'm a wimp. Now let me go."

Knowing he had let her best him again, she released him and collapsed on the couch. "I love you, David," she said with a reflection of softness in her voice. "Don't you ever leave me!"

"I won't, Katie," he replied grabbing her tight and holding her near. "I promise."

Chapter 14
FORMAL INTRODUCTIONS

The morning mist hung low to the ground the next day as the headlights of Katie's truck illuminated the back gate at old Fire Station 18. Just as she had done a hundred times before at the other station, Katie got out of her car and walked over to the gate and unlocked it. This time, however, something different happened; something magical.

As if she was being welcomed in, the metal clad barrier rolled silently open as Katie stood in awe. Quietly mouthing the words "thank you," Katie got back into her truck and drove into the lot. She parked the truck and got out. She darted a quick look around the yard, but still didn't see anything. She then grabbed her gear and headed inside. Just as miraculously as the back gate had, the rear door to the station creaked open on its own power, allowing Katie to pass through. Again she nodded her thanks and headed for her locker.

Arriving at the locker room door, Katie stood there for a moment wondering if it was going to magically open as the others had. It did not. As if the spirit was telling her that he respected her privacy, the solid, brown door remained closed. Katie smiled, pleased at this. She knew that if he had really wanted to, the ghost could have seen more of her than she would have preferred. No longer fearing any prying eyes, Katie quickly changed into her work uniform and began her morning ritual of rookie duties. The flag went up, and the hot coffee was made without a word muttered from Katie's mouth. As she laid out the morning newspaper across the kitchen table, she tried to think of something clever to say to her new acquaintance. No matter how hard she tried though, she couldn't come up with the first words to say to the ghost.

Twenty minutes had passed and Katie finally finished her morning duties. All of a sudden, the answer to her earlier question came to her. "Why not just start out simple and let it go from there," she thought. "Hello should work," she said quietly to herself. "At least I hope it does."

As she walked through the enclosed hose tower, a part of the station where washed hose was hung to dry, Katie looked upward, noticing a glowing figure some thirty feet up at the top of the platform. The dark, musty room was shaped like a rectangle put on its narrow end. There was no drywall on the interior walls, exposing the wooden studs that lined them. Spider webs filled the gaps at the higher end, showing the lack of maintenance. It had been years since any chief had climbed the wooden ladder to inspect the top of the tower.

Not scared anymore, Katie began her ascent up the creaky, old ladder that rose up through the darkness. Nervousness and exhilaration traded back and forth in her consciousness as she neared ever closer to the specter. Reaching the top rung, Katie pulled herself up onto the platform and then stopped. She peered across the landing, staring in utter disbelief at the ghost of Jim Kilpatrick. From the book the other night, she had seen what he had looked like in life, but that was many years ago, and the spirit world had changed him. His puffy, pimple filled cheeks had lost some of their fullness, taking on a more drawn, thin appearance. His frame was still stout though, yet the years of loneliness had slightly bent his posture forward, taking some of his true size away.

For a moment neither of them spoke, each pondering their next move. After a slight stalemate, Katie finally decided to break the silence. Sticking to her original plan,

Katie began the conversation simply.

"Hello, Jim," she said respectfully, her not wanting to sound too familiar to him.

The ghost of Jim Kilpatrick winced at this. He had not heard his name spoken in many years, and the fact that Katie had known his identity set him back a bit.

Sensing his reluctance, Katie took one step back.

"I am sorry if I offended you by calling you by your first name," she replied, looking into his eyes. "I meant no disrespect."

"You did not," the specter quickly answered. "You just surprised me, and I am not easily taken aback."

"So, may I call you Jim?" asked Katie, stepping nearer to him.

"Yes of course," he replied. "If I may call you Katie?"

"Yes," she answered. "That would be fine."

The two smiled, feeling a new bond developing.

"So, you know who I am," Jim said, more confidently. "I guess I must be required reading in the academy, under the subject of "what not to do."

Katie felt the shame grow in him. She had read the accounts of the incident, but they did not detail everything, especially what really happened.

"That is not true, Jim. Actually, I just found out your name last night. Of course I have heard rumors since coming to this station, although, to me, they are just that—rumors."

Jim bowed his head. "They're not just rumors, Katie." His formation settled to the floor of the platform. "I would give anything to tell you different, but they are all true. No one is to blame for my death except me."

A look of understanding washed across Katie's face as Jim continued with his story.

"I panicked. I don't know what else to say. I didn't mean to. I just couldn't help myself. It was so hot. They tried to stop me, but they couldn't. I left my position, my crew, and my duty. And for this I was rightfully condemned."

The guilt continued to engulf his soul as Katie moved towards him.

"No, Jim. You're wrong," she replied with conviction in her voice. "That is not what condemned you."

"What do you mean?" he snapped back. "I left them. I dropped that hose line and ran. I didn't care what happened to them. I just wanted out. And in doing so, I not only ruined my reputation and that of my family, but I also destroyed the careers of my co-workers."

He was partially correct in his statement. After Jim's death, blame was handed out in all directions. Captain Briggs never fully recovered from the incident. He had felt the burden of command at its heaviest, feeling that Jim was his responsibility, and that he should have been able to prevent his tragic death. He retired soon after the incident. Firefighter Forbes did not retire, but he was never the same. With the memory of the fire weighing heavily on him, he eventually transferred from old Station 18, never seeking promotion to a higher rank.

Katie shook her head. She had thought about Jim's situation all night long. She even did some research into other recorded haunts, and she could only come to one conclusion for his eternal entrapment.

"I know you think your past actions are responsible for you still being here, but you're wrong, Jim. It's not your actions at that particular fire keeping you prisoner." Katie paused for effect, taking a deep breath. "It's your fear. Fear of life itself, and fear of the unknown."

Finishing, Katie let her words soak in deep. She could tell by his expression change that she had probably struck a familiar cord within him, and that deep down inside he had known the answer to his dilemma long ago. Letting a little more time pass, Katie waited patiently for his response. What she would hear next would tie her even closer to his fate—blood close in fact.

Chapter 15
FAMILY TIES

"You are right, Katie," the ghost of Jim Kilpatrick replied. "About the fear, about life, pretty much about everything, I guess. Yet, there is one thing even you don't know. I admit, I do lack the courage to move on, but even if I had it, I still couldn't do it. You see, I need someone else's bravery to help me. I can't explain why, but I know this to be true. In addition, it can't be just any Joe off the street. It must be a relative of mine; a blood relative."

Katie thought for a moment, thinking it all made sense.

"Well, that shouldn't be too hard to find," she said slapping her hands together as if readying herself for the search. "There must be a Kilpatrick alive somewhere in this city that we can track down."

"You're right, Katie, there is. And nearer than you might think," Jim replied suspiciously.

A feeling of warmth immediately started building on her stomach. Feeling this strange sensation, Katie quickly pulled her shirt up, exposing the heart-shape birthmark of her youth. It pulsated red, glowing with intensity. Then, as if fate had played its last cruel card, she raised her head to see the ghost mirroring her actions. She quickly noticed the same identical mark on Jim, its size and shape matching in every appearance.

"You see, my niece," Jim began, stating their relation. "Your father was my younger brother. After my death, he changed his name hoping to escape the name of a coward. I guess he never told you the truth. Didn't you ever wonder why he didn't want you to be firefighter?"

Katie thought back to when she had first informed her father of her choice of careers. Jim was right, he was not happy about it. He tried for months to talk her out of it, but this only fueled her desire more. He eventually tired and gave up, knowing that it was in her blood and that he couldn't change the past. Unfortunately, he died a short time after this, never getting a chance to tell her of her long family legacy in the department, and he especially didn't mention his brother Jim.

"Funny how life is," Jim said somberly. "He was so ashamed of me in life, but his death allowed you to come to me. If he were alive today, he would have never have permitted you to work at this station. Who knows, death has a way of changing you. Maybe, just maybe, he is trying to tell me something. God sure works in mysterious ways."

"He sure does," she replied. "Now, the question is, how are we going to work out your situation? I'm not exactly sure how I can help you. How do you give someone else your bravery, especially someone who's been dead for a few decades?"

Jim pondered the question. Even though it had been on his mind since his death, he had never given the details too much thought. "Well, to be honest with you, Katie, I'm not sure myself on how to go about it. It's not like when you die they give you a handbook or anything. I guess we'll just have to wing it."

"Okay," replied Katie. "I will help you, but I can't do it on my own. I'll need the help of everyone here, and that will mean an attitude change on your part. No more tricks. You got it!"

Embarrassed about his past behavior, the white, glowing outline of Jim's ghostly body changed to a faint shade of red.

"I'll behave," Jim reluctantly promised. "But, you have to keep Twiddle Dee and Dumb away from me," referring to Firefighter Rodriguez and Dunn.

"I'll do my best," she answered. "Now I have to go and try and explain things to the captains and hope they don't throw me right into a straight jacket. Also, let's keep our family's tie between you and me for now. I need this job and I don't want anything clouding my superior's judgment."

Slightly hurt by her last comment, but understanding her situation, Jim nodded his head in agreement. Katie then said goodbye and started to make her way to the ladder for the downward climb.

However, just as if mentioning their names were enough to bring them around, Benny and Tony answered the bell for round three of their fight with the ghost, and this time they came prepared for battle. Katie felt it first. The warm, burning feeling around her birthmark was suddenly replaced with a cold, wet, drenching sensation. Katie looked down to find Benny and Tony up to their old tricks. Looking for a little revenge, they had pulled an inch and a half hose line into the tower and proceeded to open it fully.

"Don't worry, Katie," Tony yelled out. "We got it now. We'll wash it right down the drain," referring to Jim as if he were a stain that could be easily washed away.

Katie watched helplessly as the once gentle appearance of her dead relative, transform quickly into that of a fiery predator. Like brimstone falling from heaven, Jim's ghostly presence swooped down upon the threat. Fear instantly paralyzed the two jokers again as they prepared for the assault.

"No Jim," Katie screamed, trying to prevent the massacre. "Don't hurt them. You promised."

Fortunately for the two tricksters, her plea for mercy worked. Just seconds before Jim reached the two firefighters, the angered specter veered sideways, passing effortlessly through the wall of the tower and vanished. Katie smiled, relieved that there was some human compassion left in her dead relative. She looked down to find Benny and Tony in a couched position, still anticipating the assault from above.

"You guys can get up now," Katie called down to her co-workers. "The boogie man is gone."

Hearing the all clear sign, the two veteran firefighters slowly lifted their heads, thanking God that they were still attached.

"What happened?" Tony questioned first. "Where did he go?"

Not realizing the fact that Katie had saved their bacon, Benny's macho persona kicked into high gear.

"I'll tell you what happened," he began, thrusting his chest out like a rooster on a farm. "We came, we saw, and we kicked some spirit butt!"

Tony, always being the follower, fell right in track with Benny's belief.

"We did?" Tony first replied cautiously. Then realizing he was safe, he quickly flopped his position. "Yeah, we did, didn't we!"

Knowing the two couldn't fight their way out of a wet paper sack, Katie just shook her head as she made her way down the tower. Reaching the bottom without slipping off one of the wet rungs, compliments of her two stupefied heroes, she passed by the two firefighters as they danced around in the courtyard, celebrating their undeserved victory. Without saying another word to them, she then preceded to the captain's office to plead her uncle's case.

Chapter 16
LUNCH GUEST

The lunch bell rang and as usual, Benny and Tony dropped the television remote control they had been battling over for the past half hour and ran to the kitchen. Instead of helping in the kitchen as they should have been, the two were busy, locked in the same old argument that had been occurring every day since the two men had starting working with each other. Their timeless battle was for supremacy of the tube. The mini wars were caused by their different tastes in television programming, not that the average person could tell the difference between the two. Tony, on one hand, loved the courtroom type shows that displayed for the entire world how moronic some people could be. Benny, on the other hand, loved the other form of brainless entertainment—the morning talk show. The morning ritual of theirs did have its benefit. The two men were always easy to find. All one had to do was look in the rec room.

Even if Tony and Benny wanted to help in the kitchen as most firefighters do, they still wouldn't be permitted. Again, the reasons for both their exiles from food preparation were as simple as they were. Tony's reason was he just couldn't cook. When he was a rookie, he was given the straightforward task of making tuna fish sandwiches. The job sounded simple enough to him and he ran with it. Things were going pretty well too, that is, up until the time he ran out of mayonnaise. That was when things turned from good to bad. Not wanting to admit defeat, Tony searched high and low throughout the station, not asking anyone for help. After an exhausting five-minute search, he simply gave up.

Then, more like a dust storm than a brainstorm, it suddenly hit him. Why not just use lard. It looked like mayonnaise, thought Tony, at least in color. An order was subsequently issued to shoot Tony if he ever showed his face in the kitchen prior to the bell again.

Then came Benny's reason for exile from the kitchen, and his was the simplest of them all—Benny was a pig. He couldn't help himself. Something about a glandular problem his brother had once mentioned. Wherever Benny was, food wasn't, at least not for long. Therefore, out of self-preservation, the crew at Fire Station 18 had to again banish one of their own from the cooking rotation.

With the last of the lunch bell tone diminishing in the background, the two exiles rushed through the door of the kitchen. There, they found the remaining crew of the station huddled up, encircling something. Not heeding the old warning "curiosity killed the cat," the two firefighters pushed their way forward into unknown territory, getting yet another surprise of their lives. Benny saw him first, turning almost as white as his vision. He immediately tried to retreat his position, but, the other half of the dumb-amic duo blocked his escape route. Tony never had a chance. All two-hundred and fifty pounds of Firefighter Rodriguez poured over him, causing him to collapse to the tile floor, the ominous sight of Benny's body engulfing him.

"Wha, wha, wha, what," is all that came from Benny's lips as he remained on top of his partner as he tried to figured out the situation.

A slight murmur of words traced from beneath Benny in the form of Tony's attempt of cries for help. Hearing his plea, the larger firefighter rolled over, revealing a stunned, yet somehow uninjured Tony.

"Okay, okay. What's going on here?" immediately demanded Tony. He inhaled deeply in an apparent effort to catch his breath. "Why did you run me over, Benny?"

He didn't have to wait for his partner's reply. The

white, glowing image of Firefighter Jim Kilpatrick suddenly loomed over Tony and Benny, filling their hearts with fear. This time it was Tony's turn to run, however, before he could escape, Captain Houston stepped forward and grabbed him.

"Whoa there, partner," he began, pulling Tony back to a sitting position. "Let us explain before you go running off again." He then turned towards Firefighter Butler. "Okay, Katie, since you seem to be our liaison with the after life, I'll let you do the talking."

The two firefighters sat and listened as Katie told the story of Jim's past and now present situation. Tony began smiling, enjoying the story-time provided by Katie. Benny, on the other hand, didn't even crack a grin. This firefighter, ghost, whatever it was, tried to kill him, at least in Benny's mind. He didn't care if he was the ghost of Christmas past! He wanted nothing to do with Jim, especially if it meant helping him.

After a few minutes, Katie finished her story and then turned towards her secret relative. Sensing what she wanted, Jim moved closer to the two men and extended his hand in a gesture of friendship. Tony quickly stood up and attempted to return the act, however, his hand just passed through thin air. The group of firefighters started to laugh as Tony mimicked the actions anyway, smiling as he did. Jim then turned towards Benny, repeating the same gesture. This time, however, there was no return of friendship, just the feeling of coldness emanating from Benny's eyes.

"Have it your way then, Pillsbury," Jim replied, pulling back his hand.

Benny quickly replied, "I will!"

For a moment, no one said a thing. Everyone just sat there, watching the two exchange dirty looks. Finally, Captain Keller broke the silence, ending the awkward moment.

"Okay, okay. I can see some of us need some time to adapt to our new guest. So let's eat some lunch and get on with it."

The tensions seem to dwindle after that, at least on the surface. The two foes moved away from one another, sitting at opposite tables. The crew of Fire Station 18, now plus one, began to enjoy the lunch prepared for them. Katie and the rest of her table started asking Jim all sorts of questions. Jim did his best to answer them, ever aware that Benny's burning eyes never left him.

Chapter 17
FITTING IN

It had been two weeks since Jim had come out of hiding and revealed himself to Katie and the rest of the crew. The word of the new houseguest had spread fast to the other shifts in the station, with the real possibility of the news going department wide. Fortunately, all three shifts had agreed that the secret of Jim's existence would remain a secret, at least for now. There was no need to let the outside world turn the station into a freak show, or a media circus. The work at the modern day Fire Station 18 was progressing nicely and the city workers had assured the captains that it would be only a few more weeks until they could return home. Therefore, everyone kept silent.

Now, luckily for Katie, Jim had been on his best behavior during this time and everyone had taken an instant liking to him, with the exception of one. Since the lunch incident though, even Benny seemed to tolerate Jim's presence. Katie knew this was all just an act on Benny's part, and that it was just a matter of time until he sought out revenge, but she would take the break in hostilities just the same.

Katie finished the Monday morning checks and proceeded to start on the housework. Monday morning was a busy day around the fire station. It was the day of the week that all the power equipment on the engine and truck were checked and then double-checked for proper operation. Belts were tightened, fuel was added, and it gave the crew a chance to handle the different equipment and keep familiar with them.

As Katie finished filling the chainsaw with fuel, a familiar, yet exhilarating sound filled the air.

"Physical rescue," the computer generated dispatcher's voice announced loud and clear over the station's P.A system.

The entire crew of Fire Station 18 stopped what they were doing and ran for the apparatus. Tony busted out of the shower, running down the locker room hall with shampoo still in his eyes. He jumped into his turnout boots and headed for the fire pole. Down he went, hitting the bottom floor with a thud. Being caught in the shower, Tony didn't have the chance to dry off completely and his wet hands couldn't provide the stopping power needed to slow him down properly.

With Tony now onboard, the taskforce pulled out of the station, lights flashing and sirens wailing. A Physical rescue alarm was one of the most stressful and challenging type of incidents. It could involve a number of situations. From someone trapped in a vehicle after an accident, an industrial explosion, or even victims pinned against heavy machinery. All of these types of calls take skill and experience to deal with.

The engine arrived on the scene first, finding a rolled over pickup truck, smashed against a telephone pole, the vehicle lying on its roof. Luckily, there was only the one truck involved, obviously the victim of too much machine for too little brain. Katie jumped down from the cab, and pulled an inch and a half diameter hose line from the transverse bed. Mike followed up with the dry chemical extinguisher, sitting it at the feet of Captain Keller as the skipper finished his size-up of the situation over the radio.

The truck pulled up next, the hissing sound of the air brakes being applied filling the air. Pulling the "Jaws of Life" from one of the compartments, Tony and Benny went right to work, setting up the equipment. It may be a strong fact that the two firefighters were knuckleheads around the station, but no one could say they didn't know their job out in the field.

Katie made it to the smashed truck first, bending down and peering into what was left of the passenger compartment. There, she witnessed what she thought could only have been pure divine intervention. What use to be the space where the driver sat was now a mesh of crumpled metal and plastic. Somehow though, the driver of the truck had bent and twisted his body into shapes that only a contortionist could dream of, and he appeared uninjured. Katie yelled back to Mike telling him there was only one patient inside. Mike transferred the information to the captain, and then made his way to the driver's side of the vehicle to check for hazards.

"You okay, sir?" Katie asked, sticking her head into the mangled passenger compartment from the other side.

The trapped man turned his head slightly to the right, attempting to look at who was speaking to him. Katie reached inside and immediately grabbed his head, stopping it from turning. "Don't move, sir," she commanded, quickly placing a C-collar around his neck. The "C" stood for cervical, and the hard, plastic collar was designed to keep the neck in a stable position just in case there was any unseen spinal trauma.

"Hey, what are you doing, honey?" the man slowly responded, slurring the last word. Next, he reached out, attempting to pull the collar off his neck. Katie grabbed his hands and pushed them down.

"I'm trying to help you, sir. Leave the collar alone."

The man did as she asked as Katie adjusted the collar for proper fit.

"What's your name?" Katie queried, followed by the other questions she was trained to ask to find out if the patient was mentally fit. The man responded back with his name, age and his present location. Katie quickly backed up from the overwhelming smell of alcohol on the man's breath.

"How much have you had to drink tonight, sir?" asked Katie, viewing at least five empty cans of beer in passenger compartment.

"Just one or two," the man replied hesitantly.

One or two always seemed to be the answer from someone who likely had five or six.

The sound of power tools sprung up on the other side of Katie as Tony and Benny started working on the driver's door, attempting to pry it open with the 'Jaws of life'. And that was exactly what they were. Resembling a really big pair of pliers, the 'jaws' were powered by a hydraulic motor that could produce thousands of pounds of thrust, giving them the ability to cut and tear anything they could get a purchase on.

Hearing all the noise erupt around him, the trapped

man again started pulling at the C-collar placed on his neck. Once more, Katie pushed his hands away, however, this time the man did not waver in his attempt for freedom. Confused and scared, the drunken man next grabbed Katie by the hands and pulled her forward, leaving her legs dangling out the window. She tried desperately to break free of his grip, but the man overpowered her. Suddenly, from out of nowhere, the ghost of Jim Kilpatrick appeared in the cab of the truck, startling the driver, providing Katie the needed distraction to free herself.

"What's up, my man?" Jim posed to the driver. "You're not giving my girl here trouble, are you?"

The stunned man started shaking his head, but Jim put a quick stop to this, grabbing him by the chin.

"Hey, don't you remember what the firefighter told you?" questioned Jim, staring him in the eyes. "Don't move your neck!"

The driver immediately complied, stopping the movement. Jim then turned his attention to Katie who was trying to control her laughter.

"There you go, Katie, my dear. I don't think he'll give you any more trouble."

"No, I don't believe he will," agreed Katie, giggling.

Jim and Katie couldn't have been more wrong. Unbeknownst to them, the collision with the telephone pole had punctured the gas tank of the truck, secretly releasing fumes into the surrounding area. As their attention was drawn away from their victim, the driver pulled a pack of cigarettes and a lighter from his pocket. In a second, he had one in his mouth and then lit it. Outside, Mike couldn't activate the dry chemical extinguisher fast enough. The vapors from the unseen gasoline leak instantly ignited, filling the passenger space with fire. Mike emptied the full contents of the extinguisher into the compartment, quickly smothering the flames, however, there was a large amount of fire and he feared the worst. Ignoring the danger, Tony and Benny frantically worked to pry the door open. With one last thrust of the jaws, they succeeded.

With the fire out, Mike, Benny and Tony quickly bent down to see the aftermath of the flash fire. However, with the full contents of the dry chem emptied into the small compartment of the truck, their view of Katie and the trapped victim was obscured. Knowing he had to do something quickly to get the two out, Mike blindly reached into the passenger space in hopes of reaching one of them. As he did, his hands hit upon a hard barrier, defeating his attempt.

Suddenly, a gust of wind erupted around them, clearing the area of any residual dry chemical powder. Mike reexamined the compartment, this time having a clear view of the interior. A large smile formed on his face as he and his fellow firefighter now witnessed the miracle. There, sitting as if nothing had happened, were Katie and the driver of the truck, apparently uninjured, surrounded by the protecting arms of Jim Kilpatrick.

Chapter 18

SOUL SEARCHING

With the danger averted, and the driver of the smashed truck safely transported to hospital, Task Force 18 now headed back to the station. Everyone seemed to be in high spirits, thanks to Jim and his saving powers, with the exception of Jim himself. Unbeknownst to the crew of Station 18, not all had walked away unscathed from the flash fire. Something had happened to Jim during the physical rescue, and Katie couldn't help but see and feel the change.

As the wind passed though the open windows of Engine 18, Katie glanced over at the outline of Jim's ghostly form sitting across from her in the cab. She immediately noticed that it had lost some of its luster, not obtaining the same brightness as before. Mike, who was in the cab with Katie, also noticed the change.

Hey, Jim," started Mike," You feeling okay? You're

starting to look a little pale."

I'm dead, Mike," replied Jim in a sarcastic tone. "How am I supposed to look?"

Mike shot a quick glance at Katie, seeing a concern look upon her face. He then quickly returned his attention back to Jim.

"I guess you have a point there," he answered, not able to argue the fact. "It's just that you look, well— tired."

"I'll have to agree with you on that one, Mike. I am tired, but I'll be okay."

Knowing Jim wasn't okay, Katie shot a harsh look in his direction. The ghost immediately glanced away, turning his attention to the passing road instead. The interior of the cab fell silent. For the remaining trip home, no one uttered another word. The matter of Jim's obvious deception though was far from over in Katie's mind.

The engine pulled up to the driveway of the station, and the two firefighters jumped out of the cab. Katie put her helmet on and stood in the middle of the street, lifting her hands up in a halting motion for the upcoming traffic to stop. Mike ran and jumped on the back of the tailboard, ringing the buzzer three times, which gave the engineer the go ahead to back up into the station. With all the apparatus safely housed in the station, everyone went back to what they were doing prior to the call. Tony ran upstairs in hopes of finishing his shower. Benny pulled the 'Jaws of life' off the truck and topped off the fuel and then wiped the power unit down. Finished with her work, Katie thoughts now turned to the one thing she couldn't get out of her mind—what was wrong with Jim? As fast as they had pulled into the station, Jim had again vanished into thin air. Katie began scowling the station in search of him, finding each room as empty of her supernatural relative as the first. Finally, after a complete search of the station, she gave up.

Sweaty and dirty from the physical rescue, Katie decided to try and take a quick shower and clean up. She walked over to her locker room and opened the door. To her surprise, she found Jim sitting inside. A protest quickly built inside Katie seeing her relative in the one place she thought he understood was off limits to him. Before the first angry words left her mouth though, she caught site of his condition. Not only did he look dead, he wore the appearance of someone who had been buried for a thousand years.

"I'm sorry for invading your personal space," Jim began, barely audible. "However, I couldn't let the rest of the crew see me like this or they would know."

"Know what?" Katie quickly asked, running to her uncle's side. "What is it that you're keeping secret?"

Her uncle remained silent. Katie could feel the resistance in him, as if telling her would bring doom or something upon them. She asked again, getting the same negative response. Losing patience, Katie stood up and made her way to the door.

"Where are you going, Niece," Jim asked, now with a slight panic in his voice.

"I'm leaving," she snapped. "I'm not here to play games with you. I want to help you, but I can't if you won't let me."

Guilt washed across Jim's conscience. He knew that Katie had sacrificed a lot for him and that he owed her more than this. No longer willing to keep the secret from her, he began the story.

"Most people think dying is the worse thing that can happen to you. They are wrong."

Hearing this, Katie turned around and listened carefully.

"Remember, Katie, when I told you that just before I died in the fire, I was running towards a light."

Katie nodded her head, reliving the incident in her mind as if she was there.

"Yes, I remember," she replied, a slight shiver running down her back. "What about it?"

"Well, I haven't stopped running since. But now,

instead of running toward the light, I've been running away from it. Light is life, even after death, and the farther I get away from it, the more I die."

Katie now started to understand his condition.

"You see, Katie, at the beginning of our existence we are charged with life. However, there is only so much power our souls can hold. And when the power or life is gone, so are we. Entering the light recharges us. It keeps us aware of why we are here, and Who is responsible for that. However, I've been out of that light for so long that I am forgetting this. Doing the things I've done lately, like the flash fire caper, takes a lot of energy, and I am afraid my soul is near empty. One more episode like that, and I will be finished. No energy—no soul—no salvation."

Now it was Katie's turn to feel guilty. In saving her, Jim had given up part of himself. How could she ever repay that? She had grown fond of her uncle over the short period of time they been together, and though she appreciated his sacrifice in protecting her, she would never want him to give up his eternal soul for her, no matter what the cost was to her. She was right with her maker and was ready to play the cards He dealt her.

"I don't know what to say to you, Uncle," she replied, her head down. "I owe you my life, but I ask you not to save it again. I am here to help you find the way, not the reverse. Now, you have to promise me that you will never do that again. It is time for you to stop running the wrong way, and turn around. And it my job to see that this time you're running in the right direction!"

Chapter 19
OMISSION

The next day, Katie spent the entire time with her husband David. They had done all the usual morning errands, going to the mall and department stores, Katie's favorite past time. She found a nice little top and a pair of shorts to match. David left empty handed as usually. He didn't know how she could shop for three hours and only buy one outfit. He could have bought a whole wardrobe in that time. He didn't complain much though. One, because it never got him anywhere, and two, because he always got his revenge in the end, taking Katie to the television super store. David knew that Katie hated anything that had to do with electronics. He would giggle inside as she stood around tapping her shoes as he stared in awe at the rows of plasma televisions hanging on the walls. "One day," he would say aloud, hoping for permission to buy one. "One day!"

With the best of the morning spent, the two newlyweds sat down at home for a nice lunch and talked about the previous day's events. David told her how they had three calls after midnight, none of them being very exciting. One was an automatic alarm, which they were cancelled on, the other two being simple medical calls. Katie talked about her day also, leaving out the nearly tragic details of the physical rescue call. David had enough to worry about, she thought. He knew her job was dangerous because it was his job too. Anyway, all it would do was cause a fight so she omitted some of the facts.

"So, who was it that almost got cooked?" asked David. "I heard the call over the radio. Sounded pretty hairy there for a moment."

Katie turned away, making as if she didn't hear him. This response immediately answered his question.

"Katie Butler!" he sternly called out. "You lied to me. You didn't tell me that you almost died."

"Oh, did I leave that part out?" she nonchalantly replied. "It all happened so fast, I kind of forgot. Sorry."

"Sorry doesn't cut it this time, Katie." She watched as he stood up and walked over to the kitchen window. She could see the anger building inside of him. "Not telling me is the same as lying," he continued. "How do you expect me to have faith in you if you're going to keep things from me?"

"I didn't want to scare you," she answered, this time with the truth. "You have enough to worry about without thinking about my safety."

"That's my job, Katie," he replied, this time without the anger in his voice. "That is why I married you. I want to worry about you. We're a team. I'm not only with you for the good times. I'm here to help you through the bad times too!"

The fresh sensation of why she married him flooded Katie's senses. Before he could say another word, she ran to him and jumped into his arms.

"Hold me then," she said nearly crushing him against the wall. "Hold me tight, and I will tell you everything."

David held her tight as Katie told him every detail about the call, leading up to her uncle's help. For a moment, he didn't say a word. Then suddenly, his eyes lit up. "Wow!" he exclaimed as she finished the story. "How do I get this guy on my team?"

"You have to die, dear," she sarcastically replied, giving him a stern look. "So you're out of luck. You understand me! You're not going anywhere for a long time, you promised me."

"I remember," he quickly replied, unaware he would maybe have to break that promise tomorrow.

Chapter 20
EL TORBELLINO

There is an old saying "revenge is a dish best served cold." It was funny how Benny Rodriguez had a knack for relating everything he did to food. Intentional or not, this was exactly what he had done to try to pay Jim back for all the trouble he had caused him. Unlike the other times though, he would not attack the ghost directly. No, this time he would take a smarter, safer approach and strike at something he loved, the only thing he loved—Katie.

Now, Katie should have known something wasn't right when she saw Benny in the kitchen before lunch, and especially empty handed or mouth not stuffed to capacity. Nevertheless, she dismissed it as a fluke and converged on the kitchen with the rest of the fire crew. Taking her regular seat, Katie noticed the second thing that struck her odd this afternoon. Instead of the food being up on the counter for everyone to serve themselves, this time the meal had already been evenly distributed, positioned nice and neat on individual dishes.

Steve Wish, the apparatus operator was the cook today, which meant only one thing—burritos. The guy absolutely loved Mexican food and never deviated from the south of the border menu. Katie was okay with that. She also loved Mexican food and looked forward to when it was Steve's turn in the cooking rotation. What Katie didn't know, however, was that Benny had secretly added a little of his own family recipe to her lunch; one that Katie would not find so enjoyable. Benny's father had nicknamed it *EL Torbellino*, which in English loosely translated to *Twister.* Whatever the pronunciation it would mean big trouble for Katie's stomach.

Laughter filled the kitchen as the crew began their assault on the meal. Katie took her first bite, relishing in the fabulous flavor of the lunch. Benny looked on in eager anticipation, taking delight in every bite she took. Distracted with Katie, however, Benny paid little attention while eating his own plate of food, inhaling it without even tasting it. This was very unfortunate for Benny.

There is another old saying, "If you play with fire, prepare to get burned." And Benny was about to get torched. Unbeknownst to him, Jim Kilpatrick had kept close tabs on his nemesis and had witnessed the doctoring of Katie's plate. With the grace of a cat burglar, Jim had managed to switch plates while Benny wasn't looking. Not only did Benny devourer his own practical joke, he went back for seconds. A look of gratification washed across Benny's face as he witnessed Katie finish the last bite of her meal. That look quickly changed as the silent storm within him started to brew.

"What is that?" Tony exclaimed, being the first to smell the wrath of *EL Torbellino*.

Like rats fleeing a sinking ship, the men occupying Benny's table scattered for safer ground as a green cloud of gas rose up around the self-poisoned firefighter.

"Someone call the coroner," announced Mike Phillips from a safe distance. "I think something died inside Benny."

Benny's stomach grumbled again, signaling to him that something wasn't right. He quickly turned to Katie, noticing that she appeared in good health.

"She should be running for the bathroom by now," mumbled Benny to himself.

Suddenly, the ghost of firefighter Kilpatrick appeared in front of him.

"What's wrong, Benny. Is your lunch not agreeing with you?" Jim asked with a smirk upon his face.

Panic flooded Benny's senses as he realized he had been had. "Why you!" yelled Benny, lurching towards Jim, his hands outreached. As if passing through open space, the scorned firefighter pushed through the ghostly form of Jim Kilpatrick, falling hard to the ground. Benny quickly arose with fire in his eyes, the thought of revenge driving him. Set on destruction, he again moved towards the ghost. This time, however, the fire within his belly burned hotter, causing him to immediately stop all forward motion. Without saying another word, Benny turned 180 degrees and ran out of the kitchen.

The crew of Fire Station 18 could hardly control their laughter. Even Tony, Benny's best friend, was on the ground in tears.

"We get paid for this?" screamed Mike from the far corner of the room. "Something this fun can't be called work."

Relishing in his glory, Jim floated proudly above the room, smiling at Katie as he did. She returned the gesture, knowing he had again saved her from harm. Suddenly, the grapevine rang. The "Grapevine" is what the fire-fighters call the house phone, where they received all their personal calls. Being the rookie, Katie dashed for the phone booth, reaching it just seconds before Mike did.

"Getting kind of slow there, hey, Mike," announced

Katie as she reached for the receiver, adding, "You better slow down there, old timer. I wouldn't want you to break a hip or something."

Still filled with thought of Benny running from the kitchen, Mike figured he'd let her last comment slide this time. Besides, he knew Benny wasn't the only practical joker in the station. His years on the job had taught him patience, and he would bide his time and do the payback right.

"Hello," Katie said, answering the phone.

She was pleasantly surprised to find her husband's voice on the other end.

"Well, hello there too," replied David, immediately recognizing his wife's voice. "How's my girl doing?"

A faint smile formed on her lips, signally to Mike it was not for him, however, he knew what the look on her face meant. He had worn the same one upon his face when he was first married. Giving her a playful raised fist, Mike turned away and headed back for the kitchen. Katie continued her conversation.

"I'm doing great," she replied. " I was just enjoying the endless entertainment around here. How is your day going?"

Pleased to see that things were well for his wife, David did his best to hide his true feelings from her, answering

"Fine." Yet, that was far from the truth. He was upset, and had been since the beginning of his shift. Nevertheless, he didn't want to ruin her day. He himself wasn't even sure if there was a good reason for his mood. However, though he tried his hardest, he couldn't shake the feeling of impending doom that bombarded his thoughts causing the emotion.

"What's wrong?" she asked, using her women's intuition to discover the truth. "What aren't you saying?"

For a moment, silence filled the airwaves as David formulated an answer in his head. However, he would never get a chance to reply with the truth. Just as the first words left his lips, the low hum of an alarm sounded in unison in each station, stopping his response. As if listening to it in stereo, the married couple heard the computer generated voice call out the words they both lived for, "Structure Fire."

Katie saw the stream of men flowing from the kitchen. She next heard the downstairs bathroom door slam, witnessing Benny running from the room, toilet paper trailing off his backside.

"I have to go, dear," she automatically replied. "See you at the big one!"

Not wanting to be left behind, Katie slammed the receiver down, never hearing her husband say his last words of goodbye.

Chapter 21
BOOMER

The sounds of sirens filled the afternoon air as fire trucks and engines from around the area converged on the structure fire's location. From a mile away, Katie could see the heavy plume of rising smoke just over the horizon. Captain Keller, sitting in the front seat, picked up the radio receiver and reported the loom up to the dispatch center. He next reviewed the hydrant map sitting in his lap, finding the closest fire hydrant to the reported address.

"Hey, Mike," said Keller in a business-like tone. "There's a fire hydrant right across the street from the reported address. You lay the line. I got Katie with me."

Mike nodded his head, acknowledging his skipper. He didn't need Keller to tell him that though. He was the hydrant man today, and already knew it was his responsibility to secure a water supply.

Engine 18 arrived on the scene first, finding a large, single story commercial building well involved in fire. Mike jumped out to lay the line as Katie finished putting on her gear. With little effort, Mike grabbed the four-way valve with the hose attached and ran across the street to the hydrant. Katie jumped down from the cab, grabbing an inch and three-quarter diameter hose line and headed for the building. More companies soon arrived, joining the action. Truck 18 pulled up, jackknifing to a stop. Steve Wish climbed up on the pedestal, located behind the cab of the truck and started the operation to raise the aerial ladder. The aerial ladder was an extension ladder affixed to the top of the truck. Capable of reaching up to a hundred feet in height, it was used to reach high rooftops and other hard to reach places.

With the hose line in place, Captain Keller joined up with Katie at the front door. He quickly finished giving his size up to the dispatch center, calling for five additional companies. He then began donning his face piece in unison with Katie. Without warning, a large explosion sounded from within the building, startling the rookie firefighter.

"It's okay, kid," Keller called out, his voice muffled by the mask. "It sounded like a tire or something small. We'll take it slow. Just stay with me."

If that was a small one, thought Katie, she'd hate to hear anything big. She looked up and read the sign posted on the corner of the building. "Stan's Carpet Warehouse."

I didn't know carpet exploded," replied Katie, more nervous than she had ever been.

It doesn't," answered Keller. "It was probably a propane tank on a forklift or one of its tires as I said."

Trusting his experience, Katie readied herself for entry. Another explosion sounded from inside, causing Katie to rethink the situation. She took one-step back. As she did, a pair of strong hands stopped her in place. She turned to discover her husband, David, accompanied by his skipper standing there, a hose line in his hand.

"Where are you going, little girl," smirked her husband as he pulled out his face piece.

"David!" she called out, wanting to grab him and hold him, but not daring to. "What are you doing here?"

"Fighting fire, dear," he replied sarcastically, answering the rhetorical question.

"I know that!" she quickly snapped back. David slapped his face piece over his head and turned on his air bottle. A series of beeps and tones started emanating from his breathing apparatus as it went through its self-diagnostics. Katie was about to say something else when her captain grabbed her by the shoulder and got her attention.

"Let's go, Katie," he ordered. "You have all day tomorrow to talk to hubby. Right now, we have work to do."

Feeling the pressure, Katie gave David one last smile, and then tuned back toward the inferno. David quickly pulled his hose line next to her, showing her his support.

"Be careful, Katie," yelled David over all the exterior noise. "I'll see you soon."

As the two teams of firefighters made their way into the building, Katie again looked over at her husband. A sick feeling struck her, a feeling of loss and despair. Wanting to call out to him, but knowing she couldn't, she struggled with her emotions as the ambient temperature around her rose. Half the building was heavily involved with fire. It was more fire than Katie had seen in her lifetime. Looking around, she could see large stacks of carpet, piled high to the ceiling. Rows upon rows filled the warehouse. Smoke and flames soared from them, sending thick, black smoke upward. Captain Keller grabbed Katie by the back of her turnout coat and stopped her forward motion. He then turned his attention to the other captain, saying something that Katie could not make out.

Turning back to her, he told Katie that the other company was going to head to the right, while Katie would concentrate on the left. He was quick to remind her not to oppose the other team's hose line, so that no one got steamed. Katie nodded her head, acknowledging his order. She watched as the darkness of the smoke around them swallowed the figures of her husband's team as they moved off. Trying to shake the ill feeling inside her, Katie began her assault on the flames. She pulled back hard on the handle of the nozzle, immediately feeling the surging water flow free.

Chapter 22
REDEMPTION

From the tip of the nozzle, appeared Jim Kilpatrick, shaking the water from his ears.

"Whoa, what a ride," he cried out, wringing himself dry. "You haven't died until you've been shot out of a hose line."

Katie thought about his last comment and just shook her head. Paying him no attention, she continued the fire fight, making good progress against the flames. Jim peered to the right, watching the slow progress of David's team. The ghost could see the fire load was much heavier over there and that the blaze was winning the battle.

"Hey, Jim," called out Captain Keller from behind Katie. "How's it feel to be back in your old stomping grounds. Kind of creepy the second time around, hey!"

Jim looked at him with a questioning expression.

"The building, Jim," replied Keller. "This is where you

bought it. Don't you remember it? It's just a different business now"

Jim quickly spiraled around, looking intensively at his surroundings. His memory faded through the years, Jim hadn't immediately recognized the structure where he had died. Keller's words quickly refreshed it though. Katie could feel the fear build within her uncle, making her stomach turn. Then, without warning, he vanished, leaving the place that had taken his life so many years ago. Emptiness now filled Katie's consciousness as the bond between the two broke. She could no longer hear Jim's thoughts or feel his emotions. There was nothing.

Pressed from behind, Katie was brought back to the moment by her Captain. "Katie, let's move that line over to the right. It looks like your husband could use some help."

Katie swung the line over, making her way towards the heavy fire. She could now see her husband's team, hunkered down, low to the ground, the intense heat driving them there. Flames and super-heated smoke poured from the burning material. Katie did her best to concentrate on her given job, but it was tough. She could now feel the heat her husband was experiencing. She yelled in pain, her ears burning though her protective gear. She did not give up though. She pushed herself even harder, driving towards her goal of extinguishing the fire. All of a sudden, a large crack from above echoed down. It wasn't a normal cracking sound commonly heard within a blaze. No, it was a sickening one; a dying one. The roof of the building had finally lost its fight to the inferno, surrendering itself unwillingly to the blaze. Small particles of material started floating downward from the ceiling, followed by larger ones. Knowing the situation, Captain Keller radioed to team two to get out, but, it was too late. With the last of its strength gone, the panelized roof collapsed, sending the remaining heavy timber crashing down.

"David!" screamed Katie, her voice reaching over multiple dimensions.

Helpless to do anything, Katie and Captain Keller watched as the structure collapsed around the other team. Katie turned the nozzle on the newly fueled monster, desperately hoping for a miracle, but the fire continued to rage on. With all her might, she pushed through the heat, spraying the endless amount of fire without lasting results. It was simply too hot. The fire was so intense that even though he was shielded by Katie, Captain Keller could feel his own helmet melting around him. He had no idea how she was able to handle it. Yet, the fire did not slow her efforts. She was on a mission, one that she would complete or join her husband for all eternity. Suddenly, Captain

Keller grabbed her by the shoulder and pulled her back.

"Katie, we have to get out of here. The rest of the roof is going to come down on us!" screamed Keller over the roar of the blaze.

Katie didn't budge though. She couldn't. Her husband was in there, and he was everything to her. He was her life, her love, her reason to live, and without him, there was nothing. The ground shuttered as a large piece of debris landed near them. Keller again shouted at Katie with no avail. This time though, her captain would not be refused. She would be going, willing or not. It was his job to make sure they lived another day, and he was going to do his best to ensure that. Taking her by the shoulder, the larger man grabbed Katie and pulled her near him.

"Now listen here, girl," he said firmly into her ear. "I know you love your husband, but we have to go. He wouldn't want you to get hurt for nothing, and nothing is what you can do right now. Live to fight another day. That is what he would want."

Another scream of agony echoed from her face piece as she called her husband's name for what she thought would be the last time. Then silently, as if saying a prayer, she whispered a request to her dead relative.

"Please, Uncle. Take care of my husband. Show him the way. Don't let him fall into darkness."

Feeling lifeless, she then turned around and headed for safety. Fire surrounded the two firefighters as they made their way out. Heavy rolls of carpet continuously blocked their path. Using all his years of experience, the senior captain guided them along the walls, eventually finding an exit. As they reached the outside door, Katie turned around and viewed the area where she had last seen David.

In an instance, something caught her eye. It wasn't bright at first, but it was there. Deep from beneath the burning rubble, she could glimpse a shimmer of light shining through. Her racing heart quickened further. She then watched as the light quickly built in intensity, eventually engulfing the entire pile of debris covering David and his captain. Suddenly, as if a star exploded, the piles of wood and roofing material shot outward unveiling its secret.

Katie's heart soared with relief as she viewed the second miracle in her life. Standing there, as if they were just hanging out at the fire station, stood David, his captain, and her Uncle Jim, with his protective life force surrounding them. Things were not as safe as they seemed though. Jim's protective shell was failing, along with his chance of everlasting life, and if he didn't stop soon, he would quickly drain the last of his reserves and disappear into oblivion.

"Uncle!" Katie yelled, seeing small pieces of debris piercing the barrier.

By this time, the remaining crew of Station18, along with other fire companies had joined Katie and Captain Keller at the door, witnessing the magic for themselves.

"Uncle?" questioned Captain Keller, thinking he had heard her wrong. "Are you related to him, Katie?"

Katie turned, looked at her captain and then glanced back at her uncle. At that moment, their eyes met and their souls reconnected.

"Yes, sir!" she said proudly, winking at Jim. "He's my uncle, and I'm a Kilpatrick."

Hearing this, the stunned crew of Fire Station 18 fell silent. For a moment, Katie felt awkward, not sure of what to say next. Did she just brand herself a coward by association? Maybe, she thought. However, at this moment, she didn't care. She was no longer ashamed of the Kilpatrick name. She would not continue to hide her true heritage.

Unexpectedly, a voice of support came from behind, and from the least expected source.

"Well, what are we standing here for?" shouted Benny Rodriguez, from the back of the pack. "We have three of our men in there. Let's get them out!"

A proud feeling rose up inside Katie as she realized Benny said three not two. She turned and mouthed the words "thank you" to him, thinking miracles never cease to exist. Somehow, the spirit of her dead uncle had overpowered the greatest of critics, Benny, turning him from foe to friend. Soon, commotion broke out all around Katie as the other firefighters readied themselves for battle. The overwhelming support filled Katie's spirit, re-energizing her desire for life and giving Jim the extra power needed to hold on a short time more.

Unfortunately though, as the team of firefighters moved in for the rescue, the hopelessness of the situation became very apparent. Heavy equipment that had been positioned on the roof started falling through the compromised construction. One of the many thousand pound air conditioning units crashed to the floor, landing just thirty feet from the crew of Engine 70. Knowing the situation was hopeless; Jim turned towards David and spoke.

"Listen, David," Jim began, taking the loaded hose line from his hands. "Things are getting kind of nasty in here. I need you to listen very carefully and do exactly what I say."

Though the fire crews did their best to reach their trapped colleagues, the fire had grown in intensity and the danger had multiplied to the critical stage. The battalion chief had now joined his teams inside. He quickly evaluated the situation and calculated the risk. They were not in David's favor.

"Engine 18 from Battalion 15," radioed the chief to his fire captain. "Engine 18, I want you and everyone to pull out. We are going to heavy stream. I'm sorry, but I can't risk any further personnel."

Hearing the call, Katie's heart again went heavy. She knew what it meant for David and his captain. However, she also knew it was the right call to make. Too many lives were now at risk, and David wouldn't want anyone getting hurt for him. Reaching out to her uncle, she could feel Jim's powers draining. It was only a matter of time until he was fully depleted.

Not all hope was lost though. Through the smoke and flames, David and his captain suddenly appeared. They floated safely in a protective bubble, high above the fire, compliments of Jim. The remaining fire crews watched in amazement as their comrades passed through the flames seamlessly unharmed. Landing near the entrance, Katie rushed to her husband's side, smothering him with affection. After a brief reunion, Katie then turned her thoughts back to her Uncle Jim.

"Where's my, uncle?" she asked her husband, searching the crowded exit.

David turned toward the inferno, which was now burning with increase intensity, and pointed to the area he was trapped. Katie and the rest of her crew's eyes grew as they viewed yet another surprising site. In the mist of the blaze, Katie witnessed the redemption of her uncle. Jim stood there, fearless as he battled the blaze alone. By doing this he had ensured the escape of Katie's husband. Finally, after thirty-five years, Jim had come to realize that he did have what it took to be a firefighter—that of the willingness to sacrifice all for someone else. And Jim had sacrificed all that and more.

Observers from the outside could now see the flames breaching the roofline of the structure. Heavy, dark smoke rose up to the heavens, sending a message to God for help, but he did not answer. Nothing from this earth would stop the blaze now. Katie, along with the rest of her crew did their best from the doorway, pouring in hundreds of gallons of water in a last ditch effort to save Jim, yet, they might as well of been spitting on the fire. Suddenly, the walls of the structure surrounding Katie and her team started failing. The men and women immediately scrambled for a safe haven, but there was nowhere to go. Somehow, Jim heard the sound of the dying building and turned his attention back towards Katie. He saw the brick walls crumbling around her and knew he had to do something—fast. Drawing down to the deepest part of his soul, he gathered what was left of his life force and with one last, great effort, threw his power across the building, covering the remaining firefighters with a protective blanket of power. The incredible release of energy swept across the building like a nuclear detonation, knocking all things in its path to the floor. The blast was so powerful it extinguished the entire blaze in seconds.

A long moment passed before anything in the building stirred. Hot steam continued to rise off the burnt timber lying on the factory floor as the firefighters stood to their feet. Brushing the debris from her body, Katie lifted her head, peering over to the spot where Jim had been standing. He was no longer on his feet. Without hesitation, she rushed to his side, throwing pieces of debris out of her path as she went. She discovered him on his back, barely visible, just a faint shadow of his former self. She reached down and took his spirit hand in hers.

"Uncle," she said, tears streaming down her face. "You did it. You saved us. You are a firefighter!"

Hearing this, a slight smile formed on his lips. Unfortunately, it did not last long. The darkness was already taking hold.

"I'm sorry, Katie, about not keeping my promise about not helping," he began, "but I wouldn't have wanted to go on knowing you were not here."

A tear from her cheek fell from her face landing on

Jim's spirit. For a glimmer of a moment his form brightened, but quickly dimmed. Katie gripped her uncle's spirit and held him tight. Suddenly, a light from a hundred suns lit up the decimated structure. Like a waterfall of illumination, it streamed down through the hole in the roof, forming a perfect column of light. Katie and Jim immediately felt the life force from within it. Peace and tranquility emanated from it, filling all within sight with its gift. The light was so bright that Jim quickly turned away from it.

"No, Jim" Katie said, taking her uncle by the chin. "You are looking the wrong way again." She turned his head towards the light. "That is the way, Uncle. It is the only way. You have nothing to fear today. You have proven yourself worthy. Today, you can rest."

As if the column of light was magnetic, it took hold of Jim's spirit, drawing him to it. Katie walked along side, accompanying him to his fate. She could feel her uncle growing stronger with every step towards it. The light was now blinding, yet Jim's clarity of the situation became clearer with every step. Filled with the reassurance of forgiveness, he reached his hand out and pierced the curtain of light. For a brief moment in time, Katie felt what he felt—pure love. However, the Devine emotion was too much for a mere mortal to take in, and she fell back, landing on the ground.

"Thank you, Katie." Jim called out to her, moving deeper within the light. "Thank you for making me believe in myself. I couldn't have done it without you."

"You're wrong, Uncle," Katie replied. "You did it all on your own. Besides, it is me who should be thanking you. You have made me realize never to hide from the truth and to be proud of where you come from. You, Uncle, have shown me what is truly important in life—family."

Katie now stood, feeling at peace with the situation. She watched as her relative slowly immersed himself deeper into the brilliance. Just before he disappeared though, Katie heard her uncle say one last thing to her.

"Remember, Katie," he said, his vision fading further. "You may only live once, however, if you live it right, once is just enough."

And with that said, Jim gave her one last smile and then moved into the light and joined with it forever!

The End

ABOUT THE AUTHOR

With more than twenty years of service with the Los Angeles City Fire Department, John still lives in Southern California with his wife and children, and continues to write and share his experiences with all. Though this book is a work of fiction, the contents are realistic in nature.